CLOSE
TO THE
BONE

LUCY TAYLOR

CLOSE
TO THE
BONE

LUCY TAYLOR

OVERLOOK CONNECTION PRESS
2013

Contents

CLOSE TO THE BONE

People think Jeannie and me must'a been a coupla' lezzies 'cause of what we did to Ric Nash. Like, for a woman to get off on messin' up a guy, she must only like pussy or somethin'. Well, let me tell you, push come to shove, I ain't that finicky, and there's times when I've buried my face in Jeannie's blond bush and sucked on that tiny, nipple-like little she-cock nestled like a baby bird between her pink folds, but mostly, it was just cause I was hopin' she might return the favor and get me off, too.

Which she never did, but then that was Jeannie for ya. Always willin' to receive but tighter than my Grandma Pearl's asshole when it come to puttin' out.

The point is, I like to get off—is that some kinda crime?

The police say it was.

And the police and psychiatrists and even Pastor Lubly from over to the First Christian Church where I used to go with Grandma Pearl and the Old Goat every Sunday when I was a kid, they've all pulled these shocked faces and acted like they never seen nobody killed before.

Shocking, they mutter, and depraved, and a few words I reckon I'll have to look up if they ever give me a dictionary—which ain't too likely. They seem to think I'd rip out all the pages and stuff 'em down my throat and choke myself to death.

They *wish*.

What they mean is, they never saw a guy get sex-butchered by two chicks. In real life and on TV and in the movies, it's always the other way around.

Grandma Pearl, when she come to the jail, I heard her tell the guard, "She's crazy as a jaybird. Always was. Cost me my health to raise her. Doctor says my intestines are damn near shot, and now my ulcer's back."

Hell, if I'm crazy, it's 'cause Grandma Pearl and the Old Goat— that's what she used to call Grandpa Moore—were good examples.

Now Grandma Pearl, she woulda' made some diesel dyke, had she wanted to cross what Jeannie called the gender line. She's a broad-bottomed old cracker gal with tits like empty gunny sacks and a mouth that'd spit in your face sooner than smile. It was Grandma Pearl who hated men, maybe 'cause the Old Goat cheated on her with that colored gal from St. Petersburg, and even fathered up a little Hershey-colored pickinniny, so the story goes. I remember Grandma Pearl would see a man on TV in a bathing suit—not a faggy French suit that outlines the guy like a cellophane-wrapped banana but regular trunks—and she'd scrunch up her face like somebody was tryin' to feed her a spoonful o' shit and go, "Oh, look at that nasty ol' naked man. Ain't that disgustin'!"

My Mama, who took off when I was six and who fancied herself better'n everybody else 'cause she'd had a year of college, would say, "Don't say ain't, Mother, y'all sound like redneck trash," but she never corrected Grandma Pearl on the sentiment, only her lousy grammar.

And me, I'd be crouched down in front of the TV with my hand up my skirt, diddling myself, and wishin' I had one o' them nasty old men for me.

Oh, I don't mean to have sex with. I was a little kid. I didn't even know what it was that men and women did.

But there were no men in our house 'cept for the Old Goat, no father, no brothers, and Mama's boyfriends never lasted long enough to get to know me, not after Grandma Pearl got a hold of 'em, and til the Old Goat started his night-time visits, I might as well've been a pattern on the wallpaper far as he was concerned.

So when I was really little, I thought the nicest, sweetest thing in the whole world would be to lay my head down on a man's big hairy chest and be somebody's little girl. I remember goin' with Cousin LuAnne to see "The Hawaiians" with Charleton Heston, and there was this scene that Grandma Pearl would've hated, with Heston laying on the bed with his bare chest lookin' as broad as a Kansas wheat field and what I would've gave for a few minutes of peace and safety with my face buried in all that gold chest hair.

I was an ugly little girl, or so said Grandma Pearl, but I hoped I'd do like LuAnne and blossom, as they say, slim down and grow long beautiful red hair and have boys driving in from three counties to get a hand up my skirt.

For me, it didn't work that way. I skipped the blossom stage and grew straight into homely young womanhood.

But by then, I knew about lust and how it goes to your head faster than a Bud with a Jim Beam chaser. And oh, sweet J.C., how I lusted. When I met Earl at the Maverick Bar, he weren't much to look at, short and scrawny with thin black hair that never looked clean, but Earl, now there was a man with a hard-on and a half, and at the start, we'd screw til I couldn't half walk, so naturally, we got married.

We'd do it two or three times a day at the start. Earl didn't seem to mind me outweighing him by a few pounds, and he only complained a little when my buck teeth snagged the head of his dick now and then.

I started likin' sex real good but Earl, he seemed to like it a lot less as time went on. He cut me back to once a day and sometimes, not at all.

I even borrowed money from Grandma Pearl and went and got braces put on, thinkin' if I straighted out them rabbit teeth, I'd be lookin' more presentable. But Earl just laughed and said why didn't I get my jaw wired shut while I was at it, maybe I'd lose some weight, and he took to fallin' asleep right after dinner and pushin' me away when I tried to get in his pants.

"It ain't decent for a woman to want sex all the time," Earl said. "My first wife, she'd a been thrilled to death if we never done it at all. You must be one o' them nimble-maniacs."

I couldn't make him understand it was more than just his pecker slidin' in and out between my legs I craved, it was his skin, his hot, damp skin slicked to mine that filled up this terrible hole inside of me, but when I tried to tell him that, he just said, "Yeah, you could be a mite tighter down below, but long's you don't have children, I guess you'll do."

I didn't mean the hole down *there*. This hole was in my chest and in my gut and it ached like an empty belly and bled like a buckshot wound. I could feel it, but I couldn't find it and I couldn't never fill it up. The only thing that stopped the hole from hurtin' for a while was skin. Just skin.

And then, 'bout the same time that Earl stopped screwin' me, the dreams come back. I held them off by foggin' up my mind with liquor, but they'd slide in anyhow, and I'd wake up feelin' like the hole in my heart was the size of the Grand Canyon.

I'd dream about the first time the Old Goat did me, how he come to my room smellin' of Redman and garlic, and the way he gripped his thing and moaned like it was a length of his gut spillin' out of his pants, all swelled up and red. It hurt, oh Christ, I thought I was gonna split open clear to my tonsils and that lump of meat would smash out my teeth and wag from my mouth like the devil's tail.

"Love you, Lisa, love you so much, beautiful little Lisa," he'd whisper while he did me. It was liked being gored by a telephone pole—oh stop, please stop—but his words filled up the hole inside, so I bit my lip and didn't scream and the pain felt so damn good I wished it'd go on forever.

I was eight then.

It went on til I was seventeen and started puttin' on some pounds. The Old Goat, he didn't care for extra flesh. He'd pinch up a roll of flab and frown just like Grandma Pearl did when she saw male titties and say, "You oughta slim down, Lisa. Don't you know the meat's tastier close to the bone?"

So I tried losing weight, but it never worked. I didn't want the Old Goat not to love me no more, but I couldn't stop eating neither.

Even after the Old Goat caught prostate cancer and died, my appetite never went away. And my skin stayed just as hungry as before.

But now I'd wake up cryin' from the dream, and I'd go fill up a juice glass with whiskey and try to figure out if I was cryin' from the memory of the pain or because I was missin' how the Old Goat used to tell me that he loved me, used to fill up the hole that Pastor Lubly says is in my soul, so only God can fill it up, but that's crazy, ain't it, 'cause God don't have no skin.

Maybe I *am* the one who's crazy. Leastwise, that's what everybody says.

Sometimes I think crazy got hot-wired into my brain when I was born. I mean, at my house, we was all fluent in crazy. It was our native language. So I figure, maybe in spite of what the shrinks say, the Old Goat really loved me, but he only knew how to show it with his pecker. I don't know, because I've never understood why people are so all-or-nothing and no middle-ground, when it comes to love.

I mean, I'm not the brightest person (and if sex really killed brain cells like Grandma Pearl says, then I'd be drooling in a corner smearing my own poop on the walls), but I know love's got a lot of faces, more masks than a Halloween store. Like a demon that keeps shape-changing every time you're about to close in on it. It shifts into something completely different-looking and slithers away.

Because I loved Ric Nash with my whole heart and body, and the cops say I tortured him to death.

But the cops don't understand about love, and Jeannie, she didn't neither.

I'll get to Jeannie in a while. Right now I got to talk about Ric Nash.

Ric Nash was as beautiful as an Angel on top of a church steeple, if an angel could have a big thick eight-inch hard-on.

He was beautiful-to-die-for, like a honey-covered ham at Christmas-time, a feast so gorgeous that, no matter how hungry you might be, still you'd hafta just admire the perfection of it, just gaze and sniff and feel the juices slobberin' in your mouth, before you picked up your knife and fork and started to carve.

Like that, I loved Ric Nash. And that's love, too, ain't it?

It was back last year and Earl had fallen asleep on the sofa again. I couldn't wake him up to fuck me so I was sitting by the TV sippin' Wild Turkey and feelin' mighty sorry for myself—here with this no count man who wouldn't even touch me and watching some Jap monster flick at one in the morning. A commercial come on, and next thing I knew here's this slab of vanilla beefcake with oiled pecs what could fill out a B-cup brassiere and long gold hair like Cinderella's boyfriend, and he's a hollarin' and carryin' on about this dude whose throat he's gonna rip out two weeks from tonight, at eight p.m. at the Tampa Armory. And his name's Ric Nash, Steamroller Ric Nash, and he's one bad dude, you better believe it.

So I poured me another tall one and while Earl lay over there gruntin' and snorin', I started to wonder what the Steamroller would be like in bed. Just a game, y'know. I figured when I sobered up, I'd let go'a the thought.

'Cept in those days I hardly ever sobered up, so the next day I had me a few beers and went down to the Armory and bought a ticket for the upcoming show.

Got so I went to see Ric Nash at the rasslin' matches almost every week. Sometimes the show would be down to the Armory, other times in nearby towns like Brandon or Plant City. I'd always stand outside the dressing room and scream and clap when Ric Nash come out wearin' one o' them red or gold spangled robes, hair so white-blond it was like starin' at the sun.

When him and the other rasslers played Tampa, they always stayed at the Holiday Inn, so after the show, you could find them in the lounge, the baby faces and the heels together, all best of friends. I knowed it was fake, but I didn't care, 'cause I didn't see no way on earth Ric Nash could fake lookin' like he did. That face and that body, they was real.

I'd get a table by myself and just set and sip Jack Daniels and watch Nash drink and dance and grope the teenage ringrats and pretty soon—long about the fourth or fifth Jack Daniels—a funny thing would happen. I'd start to get real pretty, and I'd start gettin' thin. My braces, you wouldn't hardly see those once I'd drank enough, and my titties felt as full and hard as cantalopes and I'd start thinkin', why I'm just as pretty as them girls Nash is feelin' up and I'd go over and try to talk to him or one o' the other rasslers.

One Friday night, the cunt bartender told me to leave. She said I was too drunk to serve, but I knew it was just 'cause she was wantin' to have Nash to herself. I went outside and waited by Nash's black BMW.

When Nash come out a while later, kinda struttin' funny, rollin' side to side, he saw me and a grin come on his face, kind've a leer. For a second, it looked like the Old Goat's face and I musta' jumped back, cause Nash stepped real close and said, "C'mon now, sweet thang, you wanna come to my room and party?"

So next thing I knew, I was in Nash's room and there was other rasslers there, some I recognized and some I didn't and one old guy I don't think was even a rassler, but maybe a referee, and somebody pulled my sweater off and somebody else unhooked my bra and pushed me on the bed. I thought, well this ain't too bad, no reason I can't do more'n one, but I did ask could I have a little speck to drink, so King Karloff, the Mad Dog from Moscow, went out and brought back a bottle of Beam, and somebody else rolled a number.

Meantime, this bald-headed black dude was fuckin' me, and somebody else stuck his dick in my mouth. I tried to cushion my braces with my lips but the dude was movin' too fast and suddenly he yelped, "The bitch bit me!" and somebody else hooted and said, "She got teeth that'd set off a metal detector" and somebody else took over my mouth.

It went on like that. One after the other, but it didn't fill up the hole in me, not even with all that fuckin'.

All this time Nash was settin' in the corner with a hard-on the size of the state of Florida, hand-jackin' hisself, a big smirk on his face while he watched somebody come in my hair, and I'm thinkin', I'm doin' this for you, Nash, because I love you, and then the little old guy, the referee, climbed on. He tasted like last night's Maalox, and he couldn't get his dick in—I was too wet and sloppy by then—and besides the little guy didn't have much of a boner. The other guys was laughin' and cheerin' him on, but he couldn't keep it in, so finally he just squatted on my chest and commenced pullin' and a tuggin' at hisself, and this real nasty-smelling squirt of jism trickled out on my face. I tried to keep my lips shut, but some of it got in my mouth. It tasted bitter as sin, like he'd been eatin' dogshit, and the taste got in his cum.

When it was done, somebody handed me the bottle. I guzzled deep, then I went into the bathroom and tried to clean myself—I had cum on my tits and face and hunks of my hair was all stiff with it. When I come out, they was all gone except King Karloff and Nash. I swigged down somemore Jim Beam, hoping I'd start gettin' pretty again, and I said to Nash, real bold-like, "What about you? I done the rest. Now I want the best," and Nash just rolled those too-blue-to-believe eyes and said, "Shit, I don't fuck no pigs. Get your ass outa here."

I don't remember leavin' Nash's room or walkin' across the parking lot although I know I did that. I know I still had the liquor bottle, too, because at some point, I remember standin' next to Nash's BMW, and I swung the bottle at the windshield. The bottle broke and slashed my hand, and a gigantic spider web exploded over the glass. Then Nash and Karloff rushed out of the room, and I swung the busted bottle back and forth and started runnin' around the BMW, smearin' my blood on the windows, and Nash was shoutin' in this really strange, shaky voice, not like his TV voice at all, and that was when the police car pulled up and after that, I don't remember much til I woke up in the Hillsborough Jail the next mornin'.

Ric Nash hadn't pressed charges, but the police got hold of Grandma Pearl, who called Earl, who said to hell with me, we was through, so Grandma Pearl come down to the jail herself and wouldn't you know, the old bitch had me Baker-Acted.

For those who've never had a friend or relative deemed seriously deranged, that's some half-assed Florida law says you can lock a person in a mental institution "for their own good" for a forty-eight hour period. I won't guess how many spiteful spouses and pissed-off parents have given payback that way.

Anyhow, I got sent to Central State Hospital, where they made me sit through A.A. meetings led by some fat dyke who talked about God. Then they give me a choice—go to jail for drunk and disorderly or do a twenty-eight day program at Hillsborough Alcohol Rehab Center.

So I figured, well, I'll get three hots and a cot, and I won't hafta hear Grandma Pearl bitch, so why not, there's worse deals I could get. They told me there'd be a TV room at HARC, so I figured I could watch Ric Nash come Saturday night.

Well, let me tell you, if I had it to do over, I'd choose jail.

I mean, it was like bein' at a funny farm 'cept, since supposedly you wasn't crazy, you was just a drunk or a druggie, they expected you to follow 'bout a million rules and go to all these dumb A.A. meetings and spill your guts as regular as one of them bulimic's throwin' up her supper.

And shit, never have I seen such losers. Bunch of wife- beaters and hookers and welfare Moms and one woman who'd sent her ten-year-old boy out to turn tricks on Dale Mabry Highway. I didn't see where I had nothin' in common with any of 'em.

It was at HARC, though, that I met Jeannie, who changed my life.

First time I seen her, she was rubbing up against a doorframe, sleek as a snake tryin' to wriggle out of its skin, in her too-tight-to-breathe Calvins, wearing a little black halter top pulled down to show off one shoulder. On that shoulder was a tattoo that, at a distance, looked like some kinda rocket, but up close turned out to be a little cock with Jeannie's initials tattooed along the shaft.

Jeannie was chatting up one of the counselors, and he was starin' at her tits with his eyes bugged out like somebody had just goosed him with a pool cue.

I strolled by just close enough to hear Jeannie say, "Bet you'd like a taste of this, wouldn't y'all?" in the that cum-in-my-mouth kinda voice. Then she unzipped her jeans and flashed the sucker— I glimpsed tendrils of pubic fur that looked long enough to braid.

Or maybe she was flashing me. I never asked.

Even then, I was kinda scared of Jeannie.

Something in her posture, the slink and the sass of her, the tilt to her head and her hips, the way she could say the word fuck so it had three syllables, all Jeannie's blast-furnace sexuality held this bitter, pukey aftertaste of rage. Lust and rage, rage and lust, in Jeannie they moved together like a velvet glove in a Vasolined pussy.

I never knew love and hate could get together on such close terms and feel so good.

'Cause it wasn't *me* hated men, you understand, and what the Old Goat did to me weren't really so bad. I still believe he loved me, even while he was makin' me feel like I was getting cored out with a toilet scrubber.

At HARC, you spent a lot of time in groups, goin' around the room with people sharing about all the shit that had went down in their lives to bring them so low.

I didn't want to say nothin' —my life's my own business, Grandma Pearl always said, and it was one thing we agreed on.

But Jeannie —she was a-fucking-mazing. Better than any made-for-TV movie I ever seen. Better than ten True Confession magazines rolled into one. She had stories that she must've read in stroke books or somethin'. I mean, Jeannie claimed she'd smuggled coke out of the Bahamas and turned tricks in a Tokyo whorehouse and on a yacht in the South China Sea. In Seattle, she'd been gang-banged by Satanists and left for dead, and she'd just got out of jail for slipping mickeys to her johns and cleaning them out of jewelry and cash—her stories just went on and on, til some people in the group was cryin' and some, you could tell, was just kinda scrunchin' up their jaws, keepin' in the laughter like somebody who's ate beans for dinner holds in the farts.

But nobody laughed, 'cause Jeannie was just too gorgeous and too scary.

Jeannie was beautiful like a Fourth of July parade, all color and sparks and explosion. Her hair was almost as blonde as Ric Nash's, and her eyes were alleycat green. Everybody, men and women, wanted her. I wanted to be like Jeannie and have everyone's attention, so I told about the Old Goat, even though I felt kinda disloyal doin' it.

So when I got done with my story, I said, "When I got older, him doin' me didn't hurt no more. And I know my Grandpa really loved me."

And Jeannie leaped up like her hair was on fire and shrieked, "You no-brain hick, you think your grandpa did somethin' good to you? He raped you, shitbrain! He was a goddamn child molester and shoulda gone to jail and had some three hundred pound queer core him a new asshole. Don't you see that?"

I blinked. I was scared Jeannie was gonna hit me, like Grandma Pearl used to do. And I didn't appreciate her talking like that 'bout Grandpa Moore.

"You don't know what happened, you wasn't there," I said.

"No? Look, fartface, my older brother raped me for years, and before that it was Mom's boyfriend, and some of my johns wanted to do stuff to me you wouldn't even believe—sex ain't something men do to us because they *like* us, dummy, they do it 'cause it's the best way the fuckers know to hurt us, make us feel like shit. Oh, they can beat us up, all right, but fucking hurts worse 'cause they can call it love."

That scared me worst of all. The Old Goat only said he loved me when he was doing me, but I figured that was just his way. I never thought he was pretendin'.

"Here, shitface, blow your nose," said Jeannie and offered me a tissue.

I slammed my fist into her jaw. I'd knocked Earl down one time with a punch like that. Jeannie made a sound like a dog that needs to be put out of its misery, but then she slugged me in the mouth and cut all hell out of her hand on my braces. Next thing I knew she had me on the floor and she was chokin' me, and I remember the blood dripping off her knuckles onto my face when the counselors pulled her off, and how bad my neck hurt and how *good* it hurt and how I liked being touched by Jeannie, even if it meant feelin' like my throat was full of broken glass.

After that, Jeannie and I didn't talk to each other for a while, but we were special to each other, and we knew it.

Before the 28-day program ended, we was friends. Jeannie'd let me do her nails and give her backrubs, and when Grandma Pearl brought over a box of fudge and cookies on visiting day, Jeannie was the only one I shared it with.

On graduation day, we celebrated our freedom by drivin' over the Causeway to a bar on Clearwater Beach. I got so drunk I couldn't stand, but kind of half-crawled out to the parking lot where I passed out in the backseat of Jeannie's Escort. Later, Jeannie claimed she screwed a guy in the front seat with me out cold in the back, but it mighta been she didn't tell me everything, 'cause I turned up preggers two months later, and I hadn't been with any man (s'far as I knew) since before I went into the rehab, but I never could get Jeannie to admit to nothin'. She just handed me the money to get it taken care of.

By this time, I'd moved in with Jeannie. Earl wouldn't have me back, but Jeannie, she was better than a husband, bringin' home lots of cash, takin' me out to movies and to Denny's and Long John Silver's.

Two things I liked about Jeannie: she never hit me, and she never had a pimp. Jeannie swore she'd kill herself before she'd let some woman-hating scumbag live off the labor of her ass.

Sometimes Jeannie introduced me to some guy as her sister, and we'd all three go to bed. I could never say no to her. I was too scared she'd tell me to move out, and then I'd never get to watch her deepthroat some trick's ten-incher or go around the world on a cowboy so fast and smooth it looked like her legs and arms and tongue were tied together with silk scarves.

Jeannie didn't drink as much as me, but she did enjoy her ludes and her Valiums, and she could get moody. Sometimes, when a trick was mean or wouldn't pay, she'd lude herself into a trance and start talkin' real slow and listening to sad music.

It was during one of those times that Jeannie looked at me with slitty eyes, tossed her blond hair like a baby Marilyn Monroe and said, "We oughta do us one."

I didn't understand. Or maybe I just didn't want to.

"You mean fuck one," I said, and Jeannie looked at me with such contempt I felt like I was three years old and GrandmaPearl had just discovered the shit streaks on the bed sheets.

"You know damn well what I mean," said Jeannie. "You pick. What kinda one you wanna do?"

I was scared to answer. I was afraid she'd laugh.

I told her anyways. She howled.

"You still got an itchy cunt for ol' steroid-for-brains."

I felt ashamed then, but later, when I told Jeannie the whole story of what happened, she put her arm around me, hugged me tight, and said, "Let's go get us a bottle and sit down and figure out how we'll do him."

Damn, why did I have to pick Ric Nash? I mean, I didn't hate him or nothin', he was just havin' a good time that night, but I still wanted him so much and, well, killin's just another way of havin', ain't that right?

We decided Jeannie'd be the bait. Next time Nash come to Tampa, she stood outside the dressing room wearing five-inch fuck-me sandals, a red leather skirt and a white leather bustier with her tits bulging out of the top. The rasslers kept coming out to eyeball her, but Jeannie wouldn't give them the time of day.

Right before the main event, Ric Nash come out. Jeannie arched her back so her boobs and butt stuck out like the curves in an "S" and sauntered over. They talked, then she come back to where I was sittin' in the bleachers. She didn't look too pleased.

"He wants a three-way. Me and him and his tagteam partner. We can't do both of them."

I was ready to give up, but Jeannie said, "Fuck this, if he wants my ass, he's gotta do it my way. Who the fuck's he think he is, a goddamn rock star? He's just a two-bit bleach job who couldn't make pro football." And back she went to talk to Nash again.

I knew she'd get her way, and I was right. It was to be her and me and Nash—that was the deal. I saw Nash look over at me and squint and frown, and I saw he didn't like what he was seein', but he wanted Jeannie bad.

"We're gonna meet him at the Hojo's in Temple Terrace," Jeannie said. "I told him you're only gonna watch, that you're my psycho sister. He's got coke and ludes. We'll party first."

We stopped off at a liquor store for some bottles. By this time, I'd decided it was just a game. Jeannie didn't really plan on goin' thru with nothin', but then, in Nash's motel room, after she and Nash undressed, she said, "I'll fix our drinks," and she winked at me and I thought, oh, shit, she's gonna do it, she's gonna knock him out.

"You gimme some of your sweet thang first," said Nash, and Jeannie climbed aboard his cock, which was saluting her pussy like a private in front of General Patton.

Pretty soon, she was buckin' and ridin' and moanin' fit to die, and Nash was fuckin' her from the back and pulling her long hair so hard I thought sure her neck would snap. They went at it like a pair of tigers I seen one time at Busch Gardens. I thought Jeannie'd never pry herself off Nash's cock. When she finally did, I started to climb on, but Nash just lay back, resting up like a big old Tom tuckered out from servicing a queen, and said, "Y'all just go down and make me hard again, while your sister makes our drinks."

So I squatted down beside the bed and made love to Nash's dick, which was already firmin' up, and Jeannie, she brought the drinks and let Nash taste a little off her pussy 'fore she handed him the glass.

He went out faster than I'd expected, but then Jeannie told me she'd put the knockout dose in double-strong. He kept his hard-on, though, and I climbed aboard, figurin' I'd earned this, and I rode Nash while he lay unconscious, pumping my butt up and down, and after a while, because Nash looked so pretty layin' there, I started hittin' him with my open hand, watching his head roll side to side and his cheeks pinken and his lip start to bleed.

"Stop!" said Jeannie. "These first—just to be safe."

She produced two pairs of the handcuffs so many of her tricks creamed for and secured Nash's wrists to the bed. His upper arms were thick as tree roots and corded with muscles, armoring his soft white armpits, which were shaved as smooth as a baby's tummy.

"We gonna do him now?" I asked.

"Get a loada this," said Jeannie, like she hadn't heard my question. She tugged off the dime-sized emerald ring that Nash was wearing. Then she started goin' through his clothes. She found a wad of cash and some credit cards, which she replaced, and a handful of gold chains and two diamond rings which was hid in Nash's shaving kit.

"Now let's have some fun," said Jeannie. She pulled out the switchblade that she carried in her purse in case she had to tangle with rough trade, and commenced to run the blade tip around Nash's balls and asshole. The blade made a fine white line in the skin but nothing more. She did the same with the head of his cock, caressing him as gently with the steel as she would've with her tongue.

Somethin' 'bout the way she did that made me mad, like a dog bein' teased with a biscuit it ain't never gonna get. "Lemme have the knife," I said.

Jeannie acted like she didn't hear.

About this time, Nash groaned and stirred. Jeannie tied her pantyhose around his mouth and secured his feet with sashes from two of them spangled robes. He'd lost his hard-on and was thrashing around, making his belly muscles ripple up and down.

"He's strong," said Jeannie. "Most of 'em can't even move, they got that much mickey in 'em."

"Let me get him hard again. I want to fuck him."

"Yeah, you go on," said Jeannie. "I'm gonna fuck him, too."

She produced a dildo that looked 'bout as thick as an eggplant and rammed it up Nash's rectum. Must've hurt like a bitch. His eyes popped open, zombified and spacey, and I couldn't tell if he was seeing anything or not. He moaned, and I wondered if he liked this.

You like this, don't you, Lisa? It don't hurt much.

I looked to see what Jeannie'd done with the knife.

"I had a trick one time liked to watch me fuck myself with the barrel of a .45," said Jeannie. "Another one had this thick ol' wooden snake, said he got it in Australia—damn near busted my ovary one time. Wonder what it is about men, they like to jab and poke and pry so much—seems like they can't see anything or anybody not in pain and go on and leave it be."

She twisted the dildo higher up Nash's ass.

"It's love," I said, and Jeannie looked at me like I'd started speakin' Russian. I tried to explain. "It's love because you want to know how something works, what it feels like on the inside."

That's it, Lisa. Let Grandpa put it in ya hard an' deep, so's he can feel your insides.

"If that's love," said Jeannie, "then my science partner and I musta' really loved that frog we took apart in high school."

"You don't understand," I said, and then I saw the switchblade pokin' out from underneath the sheet.

"Think about it," I said, "We could carve his cock up like a totem pole, put our initials in it."

"Right," said Jeannie, "and how about we cut our phone number into his forhead, so he can call us for a date. Y'know, Lisa, you really *are* crazy."

Then she saw I had the knife. Her hand slipped on the dildo, and the big plastic dick squeezed out of Nash's ass with a wet, nasty sound.

"Gimme the knife," said Jeannie, and I felt like, all of a sudden, we wasn't friends no more, like Jeannie didn't trust me.

"You ain't really gonna do him," Jeannie said. "You can't."

I'd never heard her talk like that. I felt kinda let down.

"I want to see his insides. I want to reach my hands way down to his heart."

Jeannie handed me a drink. I put it to my lips—shit, I was wanting a buzz—and then something told me, wait a minute, whoa there, hold on, and I poured it on the carpet.

"I don't think so," I said, and I slapped Ric Nash upside the head, hard as I could.

"Wake up," I said.

Wake up, Lisa. Grandpa's here. It's time to play the game.

I hit him again. With my fist this time. His nose cracked and then gushed. Blood ran down his upper lip and into his mouth.

He made a gurgling sound.

"Give me the knife," said Jeannie.

I couldn't hear her. But I could hear that other voice real good.

Don't cry, baby. Do this for your Grandpa, cause he loves you.

I leaned over Nash and split the smooth white skin under his ribs. Blood the color of fire engines bubbled up. I deepened the hole, discovering a layer of yellow fat above the muscle. The knife chinked on something, ribs.

Just wanna feel your insides, Lisa. Kiss your heart with the head of my cock.

"Oh, Jesus, Lisa."

Jeannie's mouth opened in a weird, silent sob. Her fear stank up the room, it out-smelled the blood and the cum and the dildo. She didn't look so hot and cocky anymore, it was like her face was foldin' in, like she was gettin' old before my eyes.

But me, I felt real fine. I felt like this is what it's like to be in charge, to have somethin' sharp and scary in your hand, and go into people's bodies, look around and poke around and leave when you good and feel like it.

I started to carve my name into Nash's belly and the knife went in too deep. Something wet and noodlish come up and then slipped off the knife tip and slopped back into Nash's gut.

I heard noisy vomiting and saw Jeannie doubled over on the floor, puking on the already vomit-colored carpet, holding her sides and shuddering. I could see the shadows between her ribs. I'd never realized how skinny Jeannie was, and right then I couldn't have told you who I loved more, Ric Nash or her, but I wanted her—to connect with her somehow—and giving her backrubs and eating out her pussy had never really made me feel connected, I needed more—oh, Jeannie, I always needed so much *more*.

She was still bent over, dry-heaving. Her naked back looked smooth and cool as a sheet of copper. I wanted to touch her tender insides and know her secret places, all of them, close to the bone, where Grandpa Moore said the meat's sweetest.

The knife sliced down alongside her spine and opened Jeannie's back like a cherry Poptart. She screeched and crumbled. I plunged the blade in over and over, until I felt the bone.

I made love to both of them for a long time. Jeannie, I think, died first and Ric Nash—well, I guess he was as tough as he claimed to be—because he lived a long time, and toward the last, he tried to talk. I leaned close, to hear what he was saying, but I'd cut out most of his tongue by then and the words came out all mushy. He said somethin' sounded like "Why?"

Cause I love you, Lisa, that's why.

But he died before I could answer.

And Jeannie, she never asked.

The shrinks ask, though. All the damned time. And so does Pastor Lubly and the prison clergyman, but Grandma Pearl, she don't ask why, reckon cause she thinks she knows the answer, that I'm crazier'n a loon. But that ain't it at all.

Grandma Pearl, she don't know nothin' about love. She don't know how it feels to crave somebody else's skin so bad you'd carve them open just to crawl inside and hide.

Because that's what I did to Jeannie and Ric Nash.

And that's how they found me, dug in deep, close to the bone, close as I could get to them two people I loved best in all the world, the people that—if there was any justice—would have been my own two parents.

Love don't have just one face to it. Love has more masks than Mardi Gras and more ways to make pain than a schoolyard full of demons.

I know, cause I been loved myself, don't ever let nobody tell you different.

ANIMAL SOULS

"If all the animals are gone, I'd rather not live," Hannah Constable said. She stared out the window toward James Peak, the fourteen footer that rose to the north of Central City. Like fine etchings in silver, the alien webs crisscrossed the face of the mountain, the metallic threads emanating from a sleek, spindle-like craft. The abomination had veiled the top of James Peak for three months now, its appearance—and that of the hundreds of other similar crafts on mountains around the world—coinciding with the disappearance of the earth's animals.

Dead, perhaps—taken for study or slaughtered for food? The cargo of some bizarre extraterrestrial Noah's Ark? Who knew?

Whatever intelligence animated the humming, undulating webs and their mothercraft didn't choose to communicate.

Hannah thought of the empty wolf pen, of Jasmine and Lupine and Columbine. She remembered the sleekness of fur, the wet swipe of tongues, the musky canine tang of them.

"You've got to eat something," said Roberta, offering her a bowl of cashew nuts. "You look like those people who came down with AIDS back in the '90s, before they found a cure."

"How can I eat?" Hannah said, "when I don't know if the animals are alive or not and, if they are alive, what *they're* eating."

"You never know," said Roberta. "Maybe the aliens will send them back. Maybe they just want to look at them."

But Roberta didn't understand the depth of Hannah's anguish. For five years, she had lived and worked at the Rocky Mountain Wolf Sanctuary just outside the Colorado gambling town of Central City. There, with funding from a government grant, she had raised grey and Mexican wolves, the latter a rare species whose numbers had been so diminished by ruthless human predation that they had been a few dozen away from extinction. She knew them better than she knew most people, their habits and eccentricities, the peculiar tremor to Jasmine's howl, the way the cub Lupine cocked her head and lunged from side to side when she wanted to play.

In addition to the wolves, there had been her beloved dogs and cats, and a dear, shaggy burro named Tonto. The animals had been Hannah's family of choice, as opposed to her biologic tribe who lived back East and whom she resolutely avoided. At fifty-three, childless, and twice divorced, Hannah had known enough members of her own species to feel, without a doubt, that the animals were superior companions.

Now they were gone, all of them. At first, with the absence of birds and domestic animals, an eerie silence had reigned. No lowing of cattle, no barking of dogs. It was short-lived, however, as the insects, now unchallenged for dominion, multiplied and proliferated. At times, even with the government's special spraying units, the day sky would blacken with the passing of locusts and Miller moths and other insects, the air seething with the buzz and the whir of them.

The seas and the rivers were emptied as well, lifeless except for the simplest algaes and sponges, another depletion which had radically altered the planet's food supply. Like it or not, the world's billions had been turned into vegetarians.

Hannah had been a vegetarian for years, so the absence of meat, fish, and poultry in the grocery stores was no hardship. But from childhood on, animals had been her friends, her surrogate children, a source of love and comfort.

In a world devoid of animals, Hannah didn't know how she would live.

"If we just *knew*," she said to Roberta. "The aliens took the animals, but for what? For food? To use them in some kind of horrible experiments...oh God..."

She could not go on. In her chest, she experienced a palpable crack, as real as the snap of a bone, and knew without doubt that the expression "to have a broken heart" was rooted in some dark, perverse physiology.

"I heard a scientist on CNN the other night say he thinks they've taken them to study," said Roberta. Reclining on the leather sofa, she chain-smoked and nibbled cashew nuts. The bowl had been full when Hannah first arrived, and Hannah hadn't touched it. Now it was almost empty.

"If they want to study life on earth, why didn't they take people, too?" said Hannah.

"Because we're human, that's why," Roberta said, as if this were the obvious explanation. "We're more highly evolved, we're...what was the word the guy on CNN used...sentient. They respect us, that's what he said. When the time's right, they'll come and talk to us, not just zap us away against our will."

"They didn't ask the wolves' consent," said Hannah. "Or my huskies' or my cats Emerald and Taj or..."

And she was crying again and shaking and would have tried to climb James Peak herself—this aging woman with a bad back and a fractured heart—but Army units had done that already, in Colorado and on mountains all over the world. The alien crafts only shimmered and spun and gave off their peculiar drone, a kind of discordant harp sound, before reeling in their webs and soaring out of reach like huge spiders disturbed in their prey-hunting.

"Take it easy, Hannah. Maybe they'll bring them back. Maybe..."

"Maybe anything, that's what's killing me," said Hannah, her sobs dry and wheezy, desiccated from an overshedding of tears. "Oh, God, Roberta, if I could, I'd trade myself for the animals. If they'd take me instead, I'd... "

"Don't be silly, Hannah. I know you loved your pets, but remember they were only animals. You're human. Your life's worth more than theirs."

"It isn't fair," said Hannah, leaning on the sill, staring at those hideous silver strands, like hundreds of ice-encrusted tic-tac-toe boards across the face of James Peak. "Humankind has treated animals abominably—hunting the whales and elephants to extinction during the 90's, letting dogs and cats overpopulate and then starve, those horrendous laboratories they discovered last year in Colorado Springs..."

She stopped, unable to go on.

"Hannah, listen to me." Roberta brushed bits of cashew off her extravagant, floor-length caftan. Voluptuous in late middle-age,

Roberta's cosmetic surgeon was to her what priests, in other times, were to the pious. Salvation, promise, hope. Boobs, belly, chin, and eyelids were all Roberta's, bought and paid for. The widow of a wealthy import-export dealer with businesses throughout the Far East, Roberta had retired here to Central City, where she indulged her love of gaming by buying the historic Teller House and spent her days entertaining visiting celebrities, occasionally belting out a ballad at the piano.

Now she put a hand on Hannah's shoulder and said softly, as though addressing a timid child, "Why do you think I asked you to come over here?"

Hanna looked mournfully in the direction of the shrouded peak. "To see that, I suppose."

"You've seen it, Hannah. Everyone in Central City has seen it. Just like the folks in Tokyo see the webs around Mt. Fuji and the people in Seattle see the ones on Mt. Saint Helen. I've got something for you. But you've got to promise not to tell a soul. Ever. Because the truth is, I don't know if what I've done is no big deal or if I've committed a crime that could jeopardize my neck."

"What are you saying?"

For the first time in months, something besides the alien webs held Hannah spellbound. Roberta was flamboyant, loud, and brazen, but she was Hannah's oldest friend, her only friend now that the animals were gone. They'd gone to school together years ago at NYU, stayed friends while Roberta went to work for an import/export firm in Hong Kong and Hannah taught environmental protection at the University of Colorado in Boulder. Roberta had first discovered Central City when she came to visit Hannah, who had just opened the Rocky Mountain Wolf Sanctuary on thirty acres of land outside the city.

On the surface, Roberta was spoiled and rich and self-indulgent. Beneath the surface, Hannah suspected she was these things, too, but what saved her from being totally unbearable was what Hannah could only think of as a thumb-your-nose-at-it-all kind of courage, the bravado of one who sees each day as just another spin on the cosmic roulette wheel, who plays the game of life with intensity and verve and not a little madness. She had always thought of

Roberta as a woman who would not live long enough to die old, and yet Roberta was old now. And smiling the smile of one who'd just spun the roulette wheel and bet the house.

"You promise never to tell anyone, Hannah?"

"I do. Yes. But what…"

"Come on then."

Roberta led the way into the second bedroom, the one she'd used as a studio during her ceramic phase. Shelves were still lines with Roberta's work. A small kiln occupied one corner opposite a potter's wheel where—

"Sweet God in Heaven."

"You like her?"

"Dear Jesus."

"I named her Spats, because of her white feet."

Hannah was on her knees at once, cradling the black and white kitten in her arms. Tears streamed down her face.

"I never thought I'd see a kitten again. Where, Roberta? How? It isn't possible."

"Almost anything is possible for the right price," Roberta said. "There's an underground in animals. Oh, the Web People or whatever the fuck they are have zapped most of them. But here and there, they missed a few and some of those they didn't get were pregnant. There's an island near Macau with animals, but Hong Kong and all of southeast Asia were stripped bare. And there've been penguin sightings in the Galapagos, except who wants a penguin, right, unless you run a zoo? Who knows how it happened or why? The Webbies missed a few. And Hannah, have you any idea what those few that they missed are worth?"

Hannah sat on the floor, nuzzling the kitten behind it's silky ears.

"What they're worth," Roberta went on, "is anywhere from two hundred thousand to a million and a half for a cat or a dog. And horses…well, if anybody ever finds one…I've heard of offers up to ten million for a nag, a mustang, a Shetland pony, anything on hooves."

"But why, Roberta? You don't even like cats?"

"You're right, I didn't used to. Too much shedding and spitting up fur balls, and none of that shameless sucking up that dogs always gave their owners. But cats were everywhere then. You couldn't give one away. But since they've disappeared, now I think back, not just to cats but to all animals really, and I see them differently. I see them as works of art. Like a Picasso or a Rembrandt in flesh. This little gal...I could watch her for hours."

"Little guy" Hannah said, checking under the kitten's tail. "But how did you get him?"

"My connections with the firm in Hong Kong. They knew someone in Macau who'd just sent three to a contact in L.A. One went to a U.S. senator, the other to the president of NBC. This one is yours."

Hannah looked up, incredulous. "Roberta, I couldn't begin to pay you whatever this must have cost. Even if I sold... "

"Don't worry about that. Just listen. You keep the cat. He's yours. Just let me borrow him back to me sometime when I want to throw a Puppy Party."

"Puppy Party?"

"Underground parties. You haven't heard? It's all the rage. Remember how in the last century when TV was first invented the few people who actually had a set invited all their friends and neighbors over. It was a big deal. The same with animals now.

Everyone *oohs* and *aahs* and takes turns petting it. You can't imagine what people do to get invited to such a thing. They're called Puppy Parties. Supposedly the president of Thailand was able to buy a mutt for a couple of million dollars and a famous basketball star was able to buy a ferret. Celebrities fly in from all over the world to gush over their little darlings."

"And you don't want to keep him yourself?"

Roberta sighed. "Of course not. He's a gift."

"God, Roberta, I'm so grateful."

"But Hannah—remember what I said. We don't know how whatever's in those webs may feel about this...if they're satisfied to leave a few animals on earth or if they're looking for the rest and won't take kindly to the people who are keeping them. They might be angry if they find you have one. So keep that in mind before you say yes. It's a risk."

"I'll take it," Hannah said, cradling the cat. "And if they come for Spats, they'll have to kill me first."

«« — »»

For the first time since the animals had been taken, Hannah found she could walk around the grounds outside her home, past the empty wolf pens, the deserted kennels and the barn, without shedding heartbroken tears.

She still longed for her animals, but now that she was guardian to one of the rarest creatures on earth—an animal that, mere months before, had been so badly overpopulated that animal shelters were destroying hundreds a day—her life had purpose, her love a tangible recipient.

Truly, she thought, watching the kitten play, he was perfection. If, as Hannah believed, human beings were tainted with innate evil, then surely animals were pure, as close to God as humans through the ages had sought fruitlessly to be.

If the aliens wanted to harm anyone, Hannah thought, why hadn't it been humankind? She'd always found the "kind" in that word bitterly ironic, considering the greed and cruelty with which her species had wiped out much of the natural world before the aliens even arrived to finish off the job.

How could anyone harm an animal, thought Hannah, watching the kitten stalk and pounce upon a ball of twine.

When it was time to feed the kitten, Hannah held Spats in her lap and offered him bits of cheese and powdered milk from an eyedropper she'd once used to feed an abandoned baby squirrel.

But Spats rejected the cheese and seemed disinclined to suck from the eyedropper. He made piteous mewling noises.

"What's wrong, baby? You don't like the eyedropper? You're so little. Probably too young to leave your Mama."

What happened next was instinct, an act that Hannah didn't consciously examine, but simply performed, an offering borne of her own longing and the kitten's need. She unbuttoned her sweater, leaned forward and unhooked her bra. Her breasts fell free, nipples puckering erect. Hannah dripped milk onto her nipple. She guided the kitten's mouth to her breast.

Spats seized her nipple, suckled. His button-sized paws kneaded her breast in the bread-making gesture of cats the world over.

Hannah bent down and rubbed her nose in the fur of Spat's head. She licked the backs of his ears, his tightly-closed eyes.

"God, I love you," she whispered.

The tiny body vibrated with contented purring.

Which was echoed and eclipsed by another vibration, infinitely more powerful, a pulsing that grew into the sweetest, most complex of chords, a harmonic strumming that Hannah felt in her throat, in the tips of her nails.

Terrified, she glanced toward the window. The alien web filled the pane like broken blood vessels in an immense eyeball.

Hannah jumped to her feet.

Spats, terrified, clawed her nipple, gouging parallel grooves that filled rapidly with blood.

The web filled the window, the room. The web became the World.

Light-headedness seized Hannah. Her vision filled with the glittering light of sun on a thousand snow banks. The alien melodies rose to keening heights out of range of her hearing, as Spats mewled with fear. To her shock, Hannah looked down and found herself bound, the webs encrusting her body and the kitten's. Her flesh, pinched by the webbing, seemed to evaporate, melt into flesh-colored fog. A soothing, limpid warmth, seductive with well-being, flowed through her.

And then, the miracle: animals.

Hannah caught her breath.

Animals.

And yet, *not* animals as she had known them. Not exactly.

Sections of web unfurled, producing other webs, more complex ones that shimmered to more artful harmonies. Inside these new dimensions Hannah could see wild beasts roaming in vast and virgin landscapes, ghosts creatures drifting like fog, ethereal, the tangible souls of every beast of the field, every bird of the air, every fish of the sea.

They moved around her like a silken tide, and of one thing, Hannah was certain: they knew no fear, no hunger, no privation. They were safe and whole and everlasting.

She looked for Spats. He was no longer in her arms.

For the first time, her amazement gave way to rage.

"What have you done?" she shouted, not knowing if her words were understood but intent on voicing them. "Why did you take the animals? How could you steal them?"

At once, the alien chords thrummed in her brain, dissolved and re-emerged as words, an unearthly birdsong that somehow rendered itself intelligible to her.

Steal them? We've saved them. We've rescued them from the barbarousness of humans.

There followed an almost unendurable slideshow in Hannah's head, testimony to the atrocities wrought by humankind on animals: the vivisection clinics, the experimental labs, the hunting expeditions that were no more than mindless butcheries...

Hannah began to sob.

At once the visions stopped. New trilling filled her head. Like delicate scalpels probing her brain, each note evoked meaning, pulled forth a word: *the animals were intended to teach humanity compassion. It didn't work. Humanity has failed.*

"But what about *my* animals? Where are they?"

The web split and replicated itself in yet more intricate designs, a cat's cradle of shifting patterns. From it Spats reappeared, then Hannah's wolves, her dogs and cats, the burro Tonto, and animals from her past as well, animals long dead, the beloved pets of her childhood.

They came to her as she remembered them, the dogs with wagging tails, the cats making serpentines of their spines as they rubbed her ankles, the wolves still regally aloof except for Lupine, who bounded after Hannah in the full joy of her cubhood.

They greeted Hannah and she bent to rub and nuzzle them and scoop the smaller ones into her arms. Tears of relief and gratitude poured down her cheeks.

"How did I get here?" she murmured almost to herself. "Am I the only human?"

You were nursing the kitten. Your flesh was joined with his, and our instruments did not distinguish. We wouldn't knowingly have brought you here.

There came a shivering in the web, a souring of the chimes into something discordant, funereal. Alarmed, Hannah struggled to escape the gorgeous strands beginning to enmesh her.

You must go back now. Forgive us.

Then Hannah was plunging through a thunderous waterfall of sound, deafened and blinded, her body disassembled and plucked back together strand by strand, her mind captive to the discordant alien song. She found herself lying on the ground outside the empty wolf pen, staring up at the sky which was gridded now with a new and ominous mesh, a vast, black netting that covered the sky horizon to horizon, its strands trembling now like a spider web in a gale.

Check for animals remaining. Final check.

In her mind, she could still hear their "words", the resonances of that strange harmonic language.

Scanning again, final scan. Only human life remaining.

And then: *Forgive us, humankind. We gave you every chance.*

For the first time, Hannah thought she understood, and terror seized her. She thought of Roberta, of her former husbands, of her parents and brother in the East. A desperate longing, to connect with her own kind before it was too late, to find love among her own species, opened in her like a wound. She flung her arms up toward the malignant web. Beseeching.

"No, don't do this! Please don't! "

Her cries were hushed into silence by one more command, the last words Hannah heard before the beginning of the final, the ultimate, extinction:

Fire!

THE BEST IN THE BUSINESS

When Arturo first awakened after the avalanche, he was in his bed back in Baton Rouge and his mother was bending over him. She smelled of Tabu and potent Mexican weed. To Arturo, her pale skin and crimson lips made an alarming contrast, reminding him of beads of blood like snow-encrusted rosebuds.

Snow. Vast canopies of it unfurling down the hillside, like someone shaking out a deadly carpet, his companions yelling at him to move and Arturo skiing, skiing for his life, except he wasn't really experienced at backcountry skiing—he was only in Winter Park, Colorado, because he had a job to do—and the avalanche kept gaining on him like a tsunami of snow and then that incredible roar, like standing on the runway next to a jumbo jet taking off, and then—night.

Night in the middle of the day.

He had never realized snow could be so black.

But his mother was here. His mother with her racehorse legs and lilting laugh and her way of stroking his cheek ("My sweet, sweet boy") as they sat on her bed, watching the afternoon soaps, which she punctuated with tidbits of motherly advice, ("You see that woman, that Melissa, she's the kind of woman to watch out for when you grow up"), and sometimes she'd let him have a sip of her tequila or a toke off her joint.

She never punished him, not even when he lied or stole, because he was all she had now that his father had run off, the only good thing she had done in her life, she used to say.

And when he got older and was too big to punish even if she'd wanted to, he discovered that, what people didn't want to give you in this world, you could take if you were just bigger and stronger and willing to hurt them badly enough to get it.

Oh no, Mama, you don't have to worry about women like Melissa. Or anybody else. The world had better worry about me.

Mama, I'm hurt.

She placed her red lips wetly on his forhead, the exact spot where you'd want to put the bullet if you were taking someone out. Her kiss made his skin tingle.

Then he remembered he was forty-eight years old and that his mother had been dead for nineteen years, and fear hopped around in his gut like an infestation of toads.

The fear quadrupled, the toads in his belly leapfrogging level with his heart, when he saw the angel. At least he thought that's what the creature was. Maudie Elway hadn't been much on religious training, but Arturo had gone to Sunday School a time or two before deciding it was for girls and sissy-boys, and Maudie had never forced him to go back.

This angel, though, was definitely not from any Bible School story, more a cross between a celestial divinity on a cathedral ceiling and a silicon-enhanced sexpot from a Fellini wet dream. In place of arms, she had a raptor's silvery wings folded across her upper body like a stripper's plumes, plumping up sufficient cleavage to display the enormity of her bosom. Her white-blonde hair—dazzling hair, sun on ice—fell in deep drifts to her naked shoulders and her pink skin captured the luminosity of palest mother-of-pearl.

The wings fell provocatively short of covering her pubis. Arturo could see the blonde fur of her pubic mound, a radiant down, and the heavy gold rings that pierced the elongated lips of her vulva.

"What is this?" he demanded. "What are you... "

The winged creature offered him a smile as bright and hard as a Times Square whore's and colder than the snow that had thundered down the chute at Berthoud Pass, burying him.

"Hello, Arturo. I'm your Fuckangel."

Arturo sputtered with confusion and disbelief. "My *what*?"

"A Fuckangel," said the being. "An idealized sexual partner, the ultimate fuck, as it were. Everybody has one pictured somewhere in their minds, that face and body that could make you hard or wet for eternity. Even the Pope has a Fuckangel, even Mother Theresa. Not even a saint can say no to a Fuckangel. But unless you're very unlucky, we only appear after death."

"Jesus," said Arturo. "The avalanche. I died in a fucking avalanche. I don't even like to ski. I was just there to do a hit on some ski bum who was balling the wrong guy's gash."

He looked toward his mother for comfort—the angel, whatever it was, was too glaring, too high-voltage sexy, she made Arturo's groin and head throb simultaneously—but his mother's eyes looked waxen, bruised, the work of a taxidermist having a bad day. Arturo had seen that look sometimes on people just before he took them out—numb, defeated, beyond terror.

Whatever it was that could put that look in his Mother's eyes, he didn't want to meet it.

"Mama, what is it? Talk to me."

She looked at him with such dread that he tried to sit up and shake her, demand an explanation, but found himself immobile, pressed back down by a terrible weight and a cold that probed along his spine like a blunt scalpel.

"Good-bye for now, Arturo," said the Fuckangel. "But don't worry. You'll see me again." She lowered her radiant head and deep-kissed Arturo's mother. A tremor shivered through the Fuckangel's body. Her wings cocooned tightly around her. When she unfurled them, the Fuckangel had transformed into an entirely different being.

"Ready, Maudie?" the new creature whispered. Its voice was male now, deep and resonant. Arturo's mother gave a tiny whimper.

The Fuckangel lifted up its wings, revealing genitals of spectacular virility, a massive phallus knobbed like a stalagmite, that bobbed against the lightly feathered belly. The gold rings that earlier had pierced its labia now clanked gently at the penetrated scrotum.

As it embraced Arturo's mother she seemed to swoon. For a moment, all Arturo could see was her black hair, tumbling into disarray under the kiss of the virile angel. The muscular flanks bucked lewdly. Arturo's mother groaned and broke into piteous weeping. It sounded to Arturo like she was pleading—for her life perhaps?—he had heard such shameless pleas before. Usually they came from some underworld hireling in disfavor with the mob or a drug dealer turned FBI informant and would begin about the time Arturo made the victim get on his knees, hands behind his neck. He always gave them time to pray. Funny thing was, they rarely prayed to any God. They prayed to him—to Arturo—their executioner. Their prayers were promises and pleas and desperate begging that he might spare their lives.

He never did. That was why he was the best in the business.

But now those same words coming from his mother's throat, *please* and *stop* and *no* made his stomach convulse and the tone of her voice changed subtly although the words remained the same, so that now *no* began to sound like *yes* and *stop* like *go on forever*.

Afterwards, the light was gone from his mother's eyes and her breath came in little ragged gasps, like something hard and jagged was struggling to pass down her birth canal, rending her as it progressed.

"Time to begin," said the angel. Its face had changed, too, the features masculine, but still coldly, glaringly beautiful, the eyes still tourmaline, but avid as a satyr, the jaw straight as the blade of an axe.

The angel gestured with a wing toward the wall opposite the bed where Arturo lay pinned down by excruciating cold. In his real room in the home of his boyhood, that wall had been papered with pictures of dinosaurs and astronauts and even, as he got older, the centerfolds his mother pretended not to see. Now it was bare and viscous grey, like the puke of an anorexic. As Arturo watched, images moved and changed upon it like the shifting shapes of clouds.

His mother and the Fuckangel watched, too. As soon as Arturo realized what they were viewing, he swore and tried to distract his mother. Jesus, she mustn't see the things he'd done! She'd loved him blindly, after all, oblivious to his appetite for cruelty. It was she who had convinced him he was special, entitled to have whatever he wanted in the world whether he'd earned it or not.

Now she tried to turn away, but the Fuckangel tilted her chin up, began caressing the length of her body. As the angel's touches grew more intimate, strange sounds emerged from Maudie's mouth, sounds Arturo found almost as sickening to hear as the scenes on the wall must be terrible for his mother to view.

Arturo was forcing a man and a woman into the trunk of a car. The woman struggled and he had to whack her across the jaw with the side of his gun to get her to go in, while the man begged and tried to make a deal. The car was white, a late model El Dorado, the landscape that of the desert outside Tucson, the banshee silhouettes of the saguaros rising up like exclamation points to punctuate the bleakness.

Arturo remembered hiding his rental car half a mile away and walking to where the two sat in their car, killing a six-pack while they waited for an Arthur Morrisett of Miami to arrive to buy four kilos of cocaine. The man was Mexican, little more than a mule, but an ambitious mule who'd skimmed too much of his boss's profits, the woman his unfortunate companion.

The woman was sobbing now, and so was Arturo's mother, but the images kept unfolding, relentless and horrific: Arturo siphoning gas out of the El Dorado's tank, ringing the car with it before he tossed the match. The El Dorado going up like raw meat on a spit and the sounds from within the trunk—had he really been able to hear the screams so clearly the first time?—as the two fried alive inside their metal coffin.

"Arturo? Arturo, sweetie? Is that an erection I see?"

He squirmed with shame, like the time his mother'd caught him beating his meat into one of her bras. At least jerking off was normal for teenaged boys. But did she guess he always got a hard-on when he killed someone, that when he torched the El Dorado his dick had been stiff as a crowbar, hot as a hound on the trail of blood? Did she guess it was the sexual rush he got from inflicting pain that *really* made him the best in the business?

"Sweetheart, I'm so very sorry," she was saying, her heart-shaped face pressed near his, the pungency of the pot smell over-powering her perfume. "I have to do this. He says I must."

Before Arturo fully realized what she was doing, he felt the surge of heat. Flames bloomed like roses in his mother's hands—she was juggling fire—as, with a cry, she tossed her gaudy bundle onto Arturo's bed. In an instant, it became a roaring funeral pyre, flames gnawing up his shins, skinning the flesh from his penis and groin, fire suckling at his neck like flame beasts nursing. He howled as the fire found his mouth, rammed its way inside and poured down his throat while tongue and gums and tonsils crisped like deli meats. His eyeballs bulged, then toasted as the flames consumed him down to charred bone and blackened mementos of flesh and still he lived and still he heard his mother weeping.

He lived. This, above all, appalled him. Anyone who charted such new territories of suffering surely had a right to die.

Yet within moments, it seemed, his gruesome injuries had healed, and the wall writhed again with its obscene images. His mother now looked smaller, older, her eyes deeply sunken wounds.

The Fuckangel kept a wing protectively around her, caressing its silky-looking feathers across her face.

Now Arturo recognized Buddy Mendoza, who had fucked over a very important Italian gentleman to the tune of about three hundred thou in '89. "Have fun with the scumbag," his employer had said, and did Arturo know how to have fun! He got out the "Handy Home Repairman's Tool Kit" that an old girlfriend had once given him on the mistaken assumption that he was good at fixing things. Well, not really. He was good at taking things apart. Which was what he did to this Mendoza creep, piece by piece, with wrenches and pliers and drill.

He had wondered at the time if he should write the Handy Home Repairman's Tool Kit company a letter of endorsement for their excellent product, including the truly astonishing potential of their Phillips screwdriver as a proctoscope.

The torturing of Mendoza, Arturo discovered, was a lot less fun the second time around and seemed to last much longer.

Through it all, the Fuckangel was fondling Maudie, murmuring in her ear, stroking aside the hair to kiss the damp back of her neck, wedding the erotic and the tender with the unspeakable and ghastly. Arturo could see her shoulder's quaver, hear her hiccoughy sobs above the obscene gurgling noises Mendoza made.

But when the scene was finally finished and the woman who had claimed to love him more than life itself stepped toward him, Arturo could only utter the kind of desperate, babbling pleas he'd heard from many of his victims.

"Please, Mama, don't. Don't do this. You don't want to do it. I know you don't."

"I must," she said. "He wants me to."

"No, you don't. You love me. I'm your son."

"I have to," she said. "I have to please him or he won't fuck me anymore," and this time he despised her for how weak she was, how pitiful, always needing a man, although he had thought he was the man she needed. "I'm sorry," she said as the wrench's strong jaws seized him like a pitbull made of metal and blood spewed as Maudie Elway began to dismantle her son.

When it was over, there was a brief respite, in which Arturo plummeted through a cold, white pain so complete and terrible, that the sheer excess of suffering left him numb. Then the Fuckangel kissed his mouth and changed into its female form, all honey and musk and curves, and licked his mutilated body, tongued his stumps and gouges. Her touch brought his body back to life, but it wasn't that she sought to pleasure him but to sensitize him once again to pain. No sooner did her caresses stir him than the agony returned, and she left him to his suffering.

During those times when the female Fuckangel wasn't with him, Arturo could watch the male version of the creature with his mother, a winged beast of indomitable virility, rending Maudie from behind, and the Fuckangel would grin at Arturo over his mother's raised rump as if to say, "She's mine now, buddy. You'll never get her back. I've fucked her wits out, and she'll never be your Mom again."

When the pictures began to show up on the wall again, the angel buried his gorgeous head between Maudie's thighs and, though Arturo couldn't see her face, he knew she watched, and she wasn't crying now at all, but shuddering with high-pitched laughter that sounded like the glee of the insane.

This time the scene showed a much younger Arturo, just out of high school, and there was that snotty math teacher Miss Arguellez, who'd called him an ignorant punk and failed him twice in algebra. He'd caught her staying late to grade papers, and he didn't just rape her—that would have been too easy, too good for her—but hauled her into the coat closet by the hair and drummed his fists into her belly until she bled inside and gouts of blood spat up out of her throat while Arturo sent her into the next world impaled on the dick of her killer.

"No, please," whimpered Miss Arguellez.

"No, please," said Arturo's mother, and the Fuckangel whispered in her ear and put something in her hands.

"Yes, I guess it would be fun," Arturo heard her say, "but why not let me do it to someone else? My father or my brother. Anyone except my son."

But the Fuckangel frowned like an angry Zeus and fluttered its great wings as though getting ready to fly away. Arturo knew his mother wouldn't be able to resist, she'd never be able to let go of such a stud, angel or not. Still he tried, he pleaded with her for mercy, but she was already at work, looping the wire around his testacles as though she'd been in the business of torture all her life.

And, definitely, she had an aptitude, for when she pulled the wire taut just as the Angel entered her, his mother smiled.

Blood-red, howling, star-spangled agony sent the pain centers of Arturo's brain into exploding overload. He bucked against the smothering weight that pinned him, bit through his lower lip so that blood squirted from between his teeth, but that pain was paltry, nothing. *Please stop.* Then Arturo's mother lifted up that part of him which was still intact, and went to work again while the Fuckangel thrust on. That tiny part of Arturo's mind still capable of registering something beyond pain and fear understood then that the Fuckangel was no angel at all, but a gorgeous demon who'd corrupted his mother down to the roots of her soul.

When it ended—Arturo babbling gibberish and biting a bloody trench in the back of his wrist—his mother was huddled weeping on the floor, arms locked around her knees, face hidden beneath the fall of hair that had gone ash-white, her front teeth chewing her lower lip into a raspberry pulp. The Fuckangel kissed Arturo quickly on the forhead and sex-changed so fast he could almost imagine the flood of estrogen rushing through her angel's blood as her penis downscaled into a clitoris, her heroic pectorals swelled to D-cup breasts.

Her smile, scaldingly bright, blazed down on him. Arturo cringed and wriggled as though skewered on her stare.

"Keep away from me," he babbled. "I know what this is. I never believed in it before, thought it was just a bunch of stories meant to scare people, but I know now. This is hell, and you're some kind of devil sent to torture me. That's it, ain't it?"

The Fuckangel laughed, a melodic trill that degenerated into a rasp. Her lovely face changed once again, became a slack-faced, leering demon. Ringlets of decomposing flesh dripped from her skull, the top of which was coming into view like an island exposed by low tide. She bent and forced a kiss like coals upon Arturo's mouth. Her breath smelled of excrement, her eyes were sightless as a corpse with pennies in its eyes.

"Wrong, Arturo," the transformed angel croaked. "As usual, you think the world revolves around you, that even Hell revolves around you. That's not the case. This isn't your hell…it's your mother's."

She smiled her reeking smile. Her coin eyes glittered.

Suddenly Arturo was plunging down the snow chute, the din of the avalanche battering his ears, the great wall of snow looming behind him, and he knew that he could no more outrun it now than he had the first time. The avalanche swept up and over him, making kindling of his legs and pulverizing his ribs, snuffing out his sight, but in the icy dark under eight feet of snow, he could still see the Fuckangel. She was in the process of transforming again. Instead of feathers, her white wings were made of icicles. Her hair was black, her full lips scarlet, her breath the familiar-as-apple-pie perfume of tequila and primo weed. "Your hell starts now, Arturo," the Maudie-Fuckangel crooned. "And remember, I'm the best in the business."

Virgin

Joey D'Angelo was standing on the corner, alone and cold in the drizzly Atlanta twilight, when the black limo came cruising around the corner for the third time. The car slowed as it neared him. For a second Joey wondered if it was that fat social worker, Ms. LaGrange, keeping tabs on him. Since he was released from Central State Hospital two weeks earlier, Ms. LaGrange had helped him find a rented room and a shit job busing tables at an omelet joint near Peachtree Plaza. She claimed to be helping him "reintegrate into society", but she was also a sneaky bitch who had a device hooked up to Joey's TV set so she could spy on him. During *Oprah*, in particular. LaGrange was always watching when he had *Oprah* on— then and whenever Joey jerked off.

One thing Joey knew, though, was that social workers don't drive around in limos. Of course, neither did most johns. Joey figured maybe this was some rich junk bond salesman or maybe even an Arab out prowling for a handjob or a blowjob. At least that's what Joey hoped the potential customer would want. He didn't do that other stuff. No way was he going to dick some pervert up the ass, much less the other way around.

He wasn't queer, after all, no fucking way. He just wanted to make some money so he could go back home to North Carolina and see his family.

Trying to look cool, Joey watched the limo out of one slitted eye. It purred up to the curb. The back window rolled down. Joey tried to imitate the other hustlers and took his sweet time, before he slouched on over.

And got his first surprise.

A woman sat in back. Pale, late 40's, hair teased up high atop her head, hips encased in slacks of some sleek, pelt-like material. She gave Joey a hard up-down, eyes lingering at his crotch with frank assessment before returning to his face. Her eyes were the color of wet, hard-packed sand. There was no warmth in them.

"Get in."

Joey didn't like being ordered around. It reminded him of his life before Central State, when he lived with his Mom and Dad and brothers and his sister Lainie, and orders, if not instantly obeyed, were followed up with blows.

"Well?" demanded the woman in her you-are-shit-under-my-shoe tone of voice. "Are you just going to stand out there in the rain?"

There came one of those moments that hadn't happened to Joey in a long time—the drugs they'd given him at Central State had seen to that—when a muted seething, like insects massing, surging, filled his head.

But it receded as suddenly as it had started.

Joey slid into the backseat.

"How old are you?" the woman asked.

"Sixteen."

He always said sixteen. He felt sixteen. That was the age he'd been when he entered Central State. It seemed like time had stopped then, like he'd never gotten any older after that. In reality, he was twenty-one.

The woman leaned back, appraising him.

"I won't mince words," she said. "I have a twenty-eight-year old daughter who's a virgin. I want you to have intercourse with her. Use force if you must, but don't hurt her. I'll pay you five hundred dollars."

Joey felt his face fall into an expression of slack-jawed disbelief, but the amount of money involved enabled him to pull himself together quickly.

"Your daughter's twenty-eight years old and she ain't never fucked?" He laughed in spite of himself. The topic made him nervous. "What is it, she's so ugly nobody wants to do her?"

The woman rapped long nails, vampire-scarlet, on the door handle. "There's nothing funny about my daughter's situation. She's schizophrenic. For years now, she's been obsessed with the idea that to save my soul and her father's, she has to sacrifice herself to God and that she has to die a virgin. She's already tried to kill herself several times. I've agonized about this, but I'm desperate now. If she loses her virginity, maybe she'll think God doesn't want her anymore, and she'll be freed from her obsession."

Joey shook his head in dumb astonishment. He was dimly aware that, at some point during her speech, the woman had gestured to the driver and that the limo was moving forward now, gliding along through rain-slick Atlanta streets.

He cleared his throat. "You ever send your daughter to one of them...them places with the pills and the shock and all...?"

"A psychiatric hospital? She's been to several. The doctors couldn't help her, and her father's given up. But she's my only child, and I'll never stop trying to help her. It's a mother's duty. I decided to bring her home and take care of her myself."

Joey felt a chill worm up his spine. *Take care of her.* He knew that feeling of wanting to protect someone. It scared him. He'd wanted to take care of his sister Lainie, too, and look how it had backfired. She'd been just thirteen, but Mom was always smacking her around, hollering at her, calling her a feeb.

"Run away with me," Joey had said. "Just do it. Run away."

But Lainie didn't want to run away with him, and when he'd tried to force her, she'd hit him in the face. That was when the noise had started, a kind of subdued sizzle that escalated to a roar, as Joey's head had filled up with what sounded like a million horseflies and hornets and wasps.

He remembered grabbing Lainie's arm and twisting it as he shoved his other hand up underneath her t-shirt, feeling the jut of her breasts, the oily sweat that ran between them as she began to struggle. He remembered striking her, throwing her down...

Vaguely he realized the woman was still speaking.

"Of course, technically, what I'm talking about is rape. Don't worry. My daughter's been in and out of so many institutions with so many crazy fantasies that she could say the sky was blue and no one would believe her."

The limo accelerated onto a ramp for the Expressway and traveled north, then exited fifteen minutes later onto Pangborn Road, where they passed the kind of stately, multi-storied mansions Joey had only seen in movies.

They went through a pair of iron gates, the limo tripping motion detectors which bathed the car and yard in broad beams of amber light. Joey saw pale adobe walls and the witchy silhouettes of moss-laden oaks flanking the gravel driveway. They stopped before a sprawling, tile-roofed home in the Spanish hacienda style. Joey got out and followed the woman inside.

"Wipe your feet," she ordered, and Joey obeyed, but the cold arrogance in her voice made the insects in his brain flutter and buzz. Adrenaline, full of anger and heat, stiffened his muscles and prodded his dick to half-mast.

"I have to lock her in her room," the woman said, leading Joey up a curving flight of stairs. "It may seem cruel, but I have to. Otherwise she might harm herself."

They entered a carpeted hallway where the woman stopped before the second door. From her pocket, she produced a key and a packet of condoms.

"Her name is Petra. She may tell you awful things about me, but try to make her understand I've hired you to do this because I love her." She gave a strange high laugh, like paper shredding. "Who knows, maybe you can even make her like sex. Maybe then she wouldn't be so quick to judge her mother."

Joey peered into the darkened room and saw a figure kneeling by the bed. He found a light switch, flicked it on.

The room was narrow and decorated all in pink, like the inside of a giant pussy. Pink canopied bed, pink walls, lamps with fluted shades that looked like giant aureoles. There were pictures on the walls, though, that didn't fit with the little girl decor, gory stuff that Joey recognized from the days when his parents sometimes sobered up enough to drag him and Lainie to church: Christ crucified and bloody, a half-naked saint punctured with arrows, a woman being stoned, another woman being torn apart by wild dogs.

The violence of the pictures fascinated Joey, so much so that it took a moment for him to switch his attention back to the woman by the bed.

She was on her knees, apparently in prayer. From what Joey could see, she didn't look twenty-eight, but closer to forty. Her hair was long, stringy, and brown, her eyes huge and opaque. She wore a billowy short-sleeved nightgown that looked much too big for her, making it hard for Joey to tell what kind of body it concealed.

"Hey," Joey shouted, annoyed that she was ignoring him.

The girl—Petra—looked up in despair. "Oh, God, Mummy actually did it. She threatened to and now she has...gone out and bought a man. She wants to turn me into a whore like she is, I suppose. To make me into the kind of harlot Daddy sleeps with."

Joey's heart was thundering with excitement and fear. He hoped the girl would freak out, really fight him, so he could get turned on. It had been so long since Lainie. The idea of sex was scary suddenly, and he wasn't sure what to do.

To cover his confusion, he took three strides across the room, yanked the cowering woman to her feet and shook her hard. No response, so he grabbed her face and pinched her cheeks together, thinking this would enrage her. Instead she gave a tiny moan and slithered to the floor.

This wasn't what Joey had expected. The mother'd said she'd fight, and Joey was primed for struggle. He'd always assumed, in fact, that it was the woman's resistance that inflamed the man's desire, that caused his cock to stiffen. He felt confused and frightened now, his dick as limp as the body of the young woman at his feet.

"Get up," he yelled.

She lay there...

"Get the hell up."

...just like Lainie did after he threw her down, after her head thumped against the corner of the iron bed and...

"Get up! I'm gonna fuck you."

But he couldn't, not with her fainted, because his cock found nothing sexy in such passivity.

"Goddamn," he said and lifted her up and whacked her jaw, back and forth, with his open hand. Nothing. He threw her down across the bed. Her head thwacked against the headboard. She didn't move.

"Oh, shit," said Joey. He sat down on the bed, trying to figure out what to do.

She came around in a few minutes. Not writhing sexily, as Joey'd hoped, but with eyelids fluttering and her body doing some kind of spastic shimmy so violent Joey was afraid that she might wet or soil herself. Christ, he'd never be able to get it up then.

This wasn't going at all the way he'd expected.

When Petra saw Joey bending over her, tears filled her eyes. She sat up and inched away from him.

"Father, watch over me in my hour of tribulation, that I may come to You in chastity and holiness…"

"Shut up!"

Joey could feel the eager stirrings of the insects, the avid jostling for position behind his eyes. The whirring of the insectile wings spoke a language only Joey could hear and understand. They were demanding blood, so he smacked the woman across the mouth. She fell back, a small scarlet rose blossoming at the corner of her lip.

"And the virgin thinketh on the things of the Lord that she may be holy both in body and in spirit…"

Her voice was tiny, like the softest of bells, yet it drowned out the black, buzzing mass in Joey's head.

"Shut up so I can fuck you."

But she wasn't stopping him. She wasn't struggling or resisting in the least. And if she didn't fight…if she didn't make him hard with her thrashing and clawing and screams, then how was he going to…?

The sound of wings in Joey's head had quieted to nothing. Inside his jeans, his dick flopped soft and useless.

Petra wiped the blood from her mouth. "Who are you? What's your name?"

He wasn't expecting that, so he answered without thinking. "Joey."

"Thank you, Joey."

"What the fuck for?"

"For not raping me."

"How the hell would you know? Maybe after you fainted, I did it."

She sat up cautiously. She didn't look at him, but at her pictures on the wall opposite the bed: gore and arrows and a rain of stones. Maybe all that weird shit turned her on, Joey figured.

"You didn't rape me. I'd know it if you had. I'd feel pain inside of me and there'd be blood."

"Yeah, well, maybe I haven't fucked you yet. That don't mean I ain't going to."

"I don't think so," Petra said. "I don't think you're that kind of man."

He whirled, teeth clenched, ready to punch the smartass bitch's lights out.

"I mean you're kind, you're good, you like women," she said quickly.

Joey considered this. It wasn't often somebody complimented him. "I liked my sister Lainie."

"Does she live here in Atlanta?"

"No, she's dead."

"Oh, I'm really sorry."

Joey shrugged. "Five years ago. She was thirteen."

"Your sister, did she die a virgin?"

"What the fuck do you care?" said Joey, remembering his sister's snatch that time he'd hidden in the closet to watch her get undressed, imagining how it might have felt if he'd only had a chance to do her before she died. "Yeah, she was a virgin."

"That's wonderful!"

Joey raised his fist. Petra fell back in anticipation of the blow, her face drawn tight with fear.

"Don't hit me. I only meant...it's awful that your sister died, but good that she died a virgin. Because she died pure, don't you see? Only virgins are allowed to enter the highest temple of Heaven. Only virgins sit at the right hand of the Father. With Jesus," she added, nodding reverently at the picture on the wall.

"What for, so God can dick 'em?"

"Of course not. God doesn't...God doesn't fornicate."

"Those pictures," Joey said, "they're pretty creepy. Why's the crowd throwing stones at that woman?"

Petra gazed at the picture almost with love. Her expression reminded Joey of the faces of the patients at Central State when they'd had too much medication. "'And the man that committeth adultery with another man's wife, the adulterer and the adulteress shall surely be put to death.' That's Leviticus, chapter 20."

"Huh? Leviti—?"

"That woman's an adulteress. She's being punished for her sins. But worse awaits her in the Hereafter. Damnation, that's the fate of all fornicators. I've tried to tell Mummy and Daddy the mortal danger that their souls are in, but they don't listen to me.

Their ears are plugged with the filth the Devil whispers to them. So I have to save them myself. I have to sacrifice myself to expiate their sins."

Joey shrugged. "Your Mom said you were crazy. I guess she didn't lie."

"Both my parents are in thrall to Satan," Petra said. "My father was arrested a few years ago for soliciting an underage prostitute. He bought his way out of that scandal, but now he has a mistress across town. My mother has a lover of her own, and now the worst of all—she pays you to come here to hurt me."

"I'm not going to hurt you. I'm only going to fuck you."

Saying it reminded him of the five hundred dollars and the night's agenda. He reached over and grabbed one of the girl's tits, thinking to arouse himself.

Petra cringed back. "Don't touch me."

Her breast was small and flat, not much larger than the tits of an overweight man. Even Lainie, at the age of thirteen, had already had big ones, tits like a grown woman. And Lainie had fought, had struggled like a wild thing.

"Shit, you're flat, but I still gotta fuck you."

"How much is my mother paying you?"

"Five hundred dollars."

Petra shut her eyes. "God forgive her. God forgive her for imprisoning me here, for subjecting me to this humiliation when all I'm trying to do is save her and Daddy's souls."

"Look, I'm sorry I gotta do this," said Joey, "but I need that money. I want to go home and see my family. See if Mom and Dad will take me back."

"Where are they?" Petra said.

"Roseboro, North Carolina."

"It must get depressing, being all alone."

Joey shrugged. "You get used to it."

"You're lucky then. I never get used to this. I never see anyone but Mummy. Daddy stays away on business all the time. I'm not allowed to use the phone or go to church."

"Yeah, that's shitty—her locking you in here." He thought about the bleak green corridors of Central State, the way it felt to watch the seasons change from behind barred windows. "I know what that feels like, being locked up."

"And I'll bet you miss your sister."

"Yeah."

The flapping of wings was hushed and quiet now. In the great scary silence inside his skull, Joey felt alone and needy and, suddenly, very small. He remembered when he'd felt like that before, years back, and Lainie had put her arms around him, comforting. *There, Joey, Mom and Dad really love us. It's just the drinking that makes them mean. They love us, Joey, really.*

"...loves me," Petra said.

"Huh?" He came back to the reality of the pussy pink room, the strange girl with blood on her face.

"Mummy really loves me," she said again. "It's just that she hasn't found God yet. Neither has my father. But God told me if I were willing to die for them and die a virgin, He'd save their souls."

"So let them go to hell" said Joey. "Why do you care?"

"Because I blame myself. When I was a teenager, Satan led me astray one night. I took some drugs and started a fire in the kitchen. I wanted to burn the house down and destroy everything. The firemen came in time to put it out, but I don't think Mummy and Daddy were ever the same. They fought a lot after that—about me and what should be done with me. Sometimes I think it was because of me they stopped loving each other. Because of me that they fornicate with other people. So I want to save their souls, even if I have to die to do it."

She smiled then, in that far-off way that told Joey some more Bible stuff was coming. 'And he offers thereof his offerings, the two kidneys and the fat that is upon them, and the priest shall place them upon the altar. It is the food of the offering for a sweet savior, it belongs to the Lord.' That's Leviticus again."

Joey thought this Levi guy must be one weird dude.

"It don't make no sense."

"They're talking about sacrifice, about giving something to God in exchange for His forgiveness of sin. In this case, the kidneys and fat of the sacrificial victim were considered the best part. So that was the part offered to the Lord."

Joey tried to absorb this talk of sin and sacrifice. He knew that he had sinned when he killed Lainie. He also knew that if he made it back to Roseboro, he wanted to tell his Mom and Dad and brothers how bad he felt for what he'd done, even if he hadn't meant to do it. He hadn't been allowed to talk to them when he was first arrested, and they hadn't been to visit him at Central State. He wanted to make it up to them somehow, so he could come back to live with them. It didn't matter to him now if his parents hollered at him. Home was home, and Joey missed it.

Petra was talking funny again, so Joey figured she was doing what she seemed to like best, quoting the Bible. "'Ye also, as living stones, are built up a spiritual house, the holy priesthood offers up spiritual sacrifices acceptable to God by Jesus Christ.' That's Peter this time," she said, clearly pleased with her knowledge. "Chapter two, but I forget the verse."

Joey realized he liked listening to Petra talk, even if much of what she said made little sense. She had the kind of silken voice made for comforting the sick, for lulling children. But this was no good, his liking her. If he allowed that, it would fuck up everything.

He jumped to his feet. "Well, you just sacrifice somethin' else to God besides your pussy, 'cause you're givin' that to me."

He reached down, seized the neck of Petra's gown, and ripped it to the waist. She didn't move.

Neither did Joey's dick.

"Dammit, I gotta fuck you. I gotta fuck you cause I need that money. I need it get home."

He pushed Petra back down and clamped a hand across her mouth and nose. Her eyes got wider, but she didn't resist. The seconds ticked. Either she was paralyzed with terror or she had nerves of steel. More seconds passed, well over a minute. Her eyes closed.

Joey released her face. He lifted her up and shook her. Her head lolled back and forth. Her eyes were open, staring at her pictures on the wall.

"Please," said Joey, "you can't just lie there like that. You gotta fight me some, like Lainie did, so I can hear…"

He was about to say, "so I can hear the insects" but he stopped himself. He'd told Lainie about the insects once. She'd said he ought to clean his ears more often and tossed Q-tips at him, giggling.

"—can't you even try to bite me or hit me or something?"

"For what? You're bigger and you're stronger. You'd only win."

"Damn right I would."

"But it wouldn't really be you winning. It would be Satan."

"Well, screw Satan," Joey said. "I still gotta have that money."

"We could fool Mummy, you know. You don't have to hurt me to get your money."

"How?"

"Go down to the kitchen. Use the key to lock me in if you don't think you can trust me. Bring back a knife. I'll cut myself and leave some blood on the sheets. You can show that to Mummy." She clutched the ripped gown in front of her. "You'd be doing God's will, Joey. By helping me, you'd be serving the Lord."

Joey thought about it. What he wanted most was the money. He wanted, too, to have sex, but Petra wasn't making it easy, not with all her talk about God. Joey hadn't spent a lot of time in church, but he believed in the God his parents used to talk about when they were sober, and that God was one mean-assed son-of-a-bitch, kind of like the world's toughest gang leader, and He'd hurt you bad if you screwed with Him.

Joey figured maybe if he could get his money and stay on God's good side, too, he wouldn't mind not fucking. Might be just as happy not to, in fact, considering that...

"Please, Joey. Will you do it?"

Minutes later, Joey made his way quietly downstairs. He paused and held his breath. Someone was crying softly. Through a set of double doors near the foot of the stairs, he could see Petra's mother silhouetted before the window. She didn't move or glance up as Joey slipped past the doors, but buried her face in a handkerchief and made tiny snuffling sounds.

Joey continued on his search for the kitchen. The house, with its vast and shadowy rooms, gave him the creeps. Being imprisoned here, he imagined, might be even worse than Central State. And, unlike Joey, Petra had no team of psychiatrists to decide that she was well now and could be released, not even a social worker like LaGrange to help find her a job and a room.

In the kitchen, he took the largest knife he could find—some kind of Japanese steak knife, so long and sharp you could probably slaughter a steer with it.

Petra whitened a little when she saw the size of it. She'd used the time while Joey was gone to put on another nightgown, a blue one buttoned high up underneath her chin.

She reached for the knife. "Here. Let me do it."

"Hey, no way. You think I'm stupid? You think I'd let you kill yourself or maybe me?"

"I wouldn't, Joey, I promise."

"Sure you wouldn't." He stepped toward her. "So how much blood do you want?"

"Just a little…here, on the sheet."

"Hold out your arm."

He could see she didn't trust him yet, didn't realize that, after his tour of her gloomy prison, he'd started feeling sorry for her.

She turned her face away. "Just a nick, where it won't show…"

But he'd already done the deed, a short shallow cut below her elbow, a place where it would be easy to conceal. He helped her position her arm above the sheet. The blood dripped down. Crimson petals.

Joey tore a strip of fabric from the white nightgown he'd destroyed and used it to bind Petra's hand.

Petra bent down and began stripping the sheet off the mattress. "Take this to Mummy. She'll pay you and get the driver to take you back to where she picked you up."

Joey hesitated. "Look, why don't you just…just come with me."

"You mean leave? With you?"

"Why not? You could come back with me to Roseboro. Your Mom would never find you."

"Oh, no," said Petra. "I can't leave here. This is where I need to be until I make my sacrifice."

"But I want to help you," Joey said. "You remind me of my sister. Not so much the way you look, but because your Mom treats you like shit. Can't you just do like in the Bible…sacrifice something besides yourself?"

"No, Joey, I promised God."

"Then I can't help you."

"No. Joey?"

"Yeah?"

"Thanks. You did God's work tonight. You came here in the power of Satan. You leave here in the service of the Lord."

《《——》》

In the Service of the Lord.

He liked that. He liked the sound of it. It gave him an idea. Maybe he really wasn't as bad as his family thought he was—a sister killer, a nutcase. Maybe he could even save Petra and pay for his sins at the same time.

Petra's mother was still at the window when Joey slunk into the room. He watched her for a moment in silence, frowning at the problem that presented itself. There was something important that he should have asked Petra, but it was too late now. Oh, well, he'd just have to do the best he could.

He came up behind the mother, holding the blood-stained sheet, and cleared his throat to indicate his presence.

She breathed in sharply and stood up.

"Is it over?"

Joey nodded.

"Was it very…painful for her?"

"No," Joey said, "she liked it. I was good. I really made her like it."

The woman's face froze in an odd grimace, as if she couldn't decide whether or not to laugh. Finally she wiped her eyes and said, "Wait here. I'll go check on my daughter and then I'll get your money. If you're telling me the truth, if she really enjoyed herself, then there'll be a bonus for you."

"Wait," said Joey. "I need to ask you something first."

"What?"

"Well, it's about…"

His hand moved underneath the sheet, gripping the knife he held there.

"Your kidneys," Joey said. "I'm not sure where I gotta cut to get them."

《《——》》

Apparently, she didn't know either.

So, after choking her, he had to search around a bit, discovering in the process that bodies were more full and colorful than he'd ever have imagined.

A treasure trove of soft, slick internal things.

At the last, though, he was pretty sure he'd got what it was God wanted. Two bean-shaped things deep in the back, that he found by tipping the woman forward so her guts poured out and rummaging around inside her torso with the knife. It was kind of disgusting, really, but then Joey figured if sacrifice was easy, God wouldn't be impressed.

Standing outside Petra's door a few minutes later, he imagined the look on her face when she saw his offering: her joy, her gratitude.

He unlocked the door and stepped inside. Petra was in the bed, curled up beneath the blanket with her Bible.

Joey held up his slippery treats for her admiration.

Petra stared. She obviously didn't understand what it was she was looking at.

"See, you can leave here now with me. You don't have to make no sacrifice."

"What…what have you done?"

A kidney slipped from Joey's grasp. It skidded across the floor like a wet, legless cockroach, leaving a trail of dark slime as it went.

"Oh, God, oh, God!"

Petra began to moan and then to scream, high-pitched and hysterically, like Lainie had done that first time—the only time—he got his hand up underneath her dress. Before she fell and hit her head…before she lay limp and dead…

"Hey, what the fuck is the matter with you? Isn't this what you said God wanted? The kidneys and stuff. Isn't that what you said?"

Petra's screams could have chipped diamonds.

The insects in Joey's head began to roil and jostle. Beneath the woman's cries, Joey could hear the frantic beating of wings.

"Hey, shut up! I only did what I thought was right. The bitch was keeping you locked up here, wasn't she? You thought you had to kill yourself for her. Now I've saved you the trouble."

"Fiend! Murderer!" Petra flung herself at Joey, punching, kicking, biting. She fought him with the strength of the demented. By the time, he'd gotten her pinned down, legs V'd, his dick was so hard it ached and the wheeling of obsidian wings made a din that hurt his head.

At the last moment, just before the swirl and flap of wings filled him utterly with blackness, Joey remembered what Petra had said about how the Lord loves virgins. He realized that, if he wanted to join Lainie in Heaven someday, he couldn't fuck this woman, however much he wanted to.

Because Petra said only the virgins sat with Jesus. Virgin, the way his sister died.

Virgin, like Joey still was.

He'd had his dick out in his hand before he realized the terrible danger. Now he stuffed it back inside his pants.

He thought for a moment and then came up with an idea. There were other things you could stick up a woman's pussy if you had to stay a virgin.

Joey reached for the knife.

CAGES

"I know what you *want*," murmured the mascara'd old woman as Loreen made her way to the stage.

Not many women, especially older, unescorted, ones showed up at Joe's Casbah. Loreen, clad only in pink tassles and a satin G-string, wasn't sure if she'd understood. She paused, and glanced back.

"I know," breathed the woman, almost a hiss. A bit of saliva flew from her parrot-red lips and struck Loreen's cheek. All around, men were clapping and whistling, but for an instant it was only Loreen and the old woman, staring like people recalling each other from some long ago dream.

Then the spell broke with a cascade of hoots and applause.

Pink tassles twirling, Loreen pranced onto the stage.

Rock music throbbed through the dark, smoky club with carnal insistence. Loreen made her belly ripple like a python digesting prey. Look at me, she thought, arching back so that her breasts shimmied skyward.

Men came forward to tuck bills under Loreen's garters. The lights made it difficult to see their faces, but Loreen was keenly conscious of their shapes and silhouettes, the dampness of their fingers, the timbre of their hoots and mutterings. She scanned the front row seats as though expecting someone special, but it was always the same crowd: horny virgins from the frat houses at LSU, rowdy bachelor parties, the occasional pervert wanting to pay $100 to suck Loreen's big toe or some other, less innocuous, depravity.

Never anyone worth looking for. Worth dancing for the way Loreen could dance.

Loreen closed her eyes to feline slits and thought of making savage, silent love with some wild stranger. Her hips returned that lover's thrusts and longing filled her, and dollar bills rained down like paper kisses.

When her set ended, she made her way to the dressing room. The old woman, her hair a lacquered dome, igloo-white, stood still as a cigar store squaw next to the bar. The pale, spittle-colored eyes locked on Loreen's. The sensation was like running face-first through a moist, ice cold spider web.

"Hold on, honey," said the woman. Her voice was rumbly deep South, magnolias and bourbon. "I need to talk to you."

A weirdo, thought Loreen. She gave a tiny, wintry smile and fled into the dressing room, almost colliding with one of the other dancers.

"Did you see that creepy old lady?"

Sedalia grinned. Her hair was blond, her skin cafe au lait.

Gold stars bedecked her ear lobes and front teeth. She was addicted to nose drops, and her sinuses drained constantly.

"Shit, gal, don't you know who that is?"

"The 'before' picture in an ad for wrinkle cream?" Loreen lowered her voice as two other dancers, an eggshell blond and a black amazon with thighs like a roller derby queen's, came in. "Don't tell me she's somebody's *mother*?"

"You ignorant," said Sedalia, wiping her nose with her hand.

"That's Daphne French."

Loreen blinked. "Daphne French is still alive?

"Course she's alive. Ain't you seen her posters all over the Quarter?"

"Sure, but I figured…I thought it was a Daphne French impersonator. I mean, that woman's got to be pushing sixty."

"Try seventy," said Sedalia, wriggling out of her red satin shorts. "They say she had half the state senators and all the local clergy in Frenchy's Place at one time or another. Plus a few voodoo priests just to cover all the bases. Here, gal, toss me them Kleenex."

"Catch." Loreen peeled out of her costume, slipped into jeans and a t-shirt. "Don't tell me that woman still dances. She looks old enough to have stripped for Huey Long."

"I went to see her dance last year," Sedalia said. "Gave me the heebie-jeebies. Her face is old, and she wears a wig and make-up laid on with a trowel, but her body—I swear to God, her body could make a twenty-year-old jealous."

"Cosmetic surgery?."

"This ain't cosmetic surgery. Ain't hormones neither. Her body's really young."

Loreen started counting out her money. "She said she wanted to talk to me. Think she's gonna offer me a job at Frenchy's Place?"

"If she do, you best to turn it down."

"You kidding? The girl's at Frenchy's Place make three times what we do."

"Yeah, and you know what they do for it."

"So? Since when did you get so high and mighty?"

"Since I decided I liked stayin' alive. Turn a trick with the wrong guy and a gal can end up smilin' through her tonsils." She dabbed at her red-rimmed nostrils with a tissue. "Shit, you of all people know what can happen. You told me about your sister—"

"Yeah, well, she was stupid. I'm tired of livin' from week to week. If I could get a job dancin' at Frenchy's Place—"

"Ain't you been listening to a thing I said? There's somethin' that ain't right about that woman. I grew up in the Quarter, an' you shoulda' heard the stories that went round 'bout Daphne French— how she took a voodoo priest to be her lover so she could learn black magic, how she did a spell one time so she'd give birth to triplets and then she drowned one and burned another and buried the third alive in—"

"Shit," said Loreen, scowling at the wad of bills in her hand, "a lousy thirty-three bucks. That's not worth climbing up on stage for."

"Loreen, you hearin' me?"

"Yeah, some voodoo crap about burying live babies. C'mon, Sedalia, save it for Halloween."

"Go see her dance sometime. Explain to me how she got that body."

Loreen shrugged. "The right lighting *does* work wonders."

"Honey, we ain't talking wonders, we're talking the Miracle of Lourdes."

"Damn, I shouldn't have brushed her off. I'll bet she was gonna offer me a job." Loreen stared up at the maze of cracks and peeling paint that crisscrossed the Casbah ceiling. "I promised Larry I'd quit the business one of these days, but it'd be great to have a chance to put away some real money."

"You been promisin' that poor fool you'd quit the business for a year now. Don't you want to settle down, do your strippin' in the bedroom 'stead of on a stage?"

"C'mon, Sedalia, guys like Larry get off on dating dancers; they don't *marry* them. If Larry likes to take me to expensive places, great, but I'm not plannin' any future. I'm not even sure he's my type."

Sedalia hooted and blew her nose. "What you mean, gal, that sweet boy ain't your *type*? What is your type?"

Loreen shrugged and tucked the money in her handbag. "Sometimes I'm not sure I know."

It wasn't just the thought of money that made her get into the cab beside Daphne French, Loreen told herself later. No, not just the hope of more money, because she didn't know if Daphne French was really going to offer her a job. And it wasn't entirely because of what Sedalia said; the girl was obviously either mistaken or exaggerating—maybe she'd only seen a woman she *thought* was Daphne French—but the old woman's words: *I know what you want*, spoken with such knowingness, intrigued her. So when Daphne French leaned out of the cab and called, "Honey, let's go have us a little drink," she went along out of curiosity.

Daphne French suggested that they go to Loreen's apartment and then barely said a word during the ride. The silence made Loreen uncomfortable, and she filled it with nervous banter about kinky customers and the brief but bone-gnawing cold of February in Louisiana.

Once inside her third floor walk-up, Loreen filled a glass with vodka and tonic water for her guest and one with straight vodka for herself while Daphne French wandered about the small apartment, admiring Loreen's fichus trees and African violets. Her perfume, which Loreen had first noticed in the cab, seemed to expand, filling the room with an overpowering floral bouquet. She found herself gulping her drink in an effort to contain her growing nervousness and nausea.

"You dance like a mink in heat," smiled Daphne French, nestled on the beige and black sofa. "Most strippers look like bored housewives humping their husbands —in their heads, they're betting the ponies or planning their next coke score. But you dance like you're coming hard enough to knock your teeth out. You got drive and you got spirit, I can tell. A girl like you, I could do a lot for."

"Well," said Loreen, "Joe gets pretty pissed when somebody quits without giving any notice, but I think three days would be enough. I could start at Frenchy's Place by Tuesday."

"Hold on now." A new formality had crept into Daphne French's voice. She drew herself up with great dignity. "I'm afraid there's been a misunderstanding, hon. I wasn't offering you a job."

"But you said—"

Loreen felt hot with embarrassment, light-headed from the vodka and the drenching scent of the woman's perfume.

"—you said you wanted to talk to me, and you liked the way I dance, so I just thought—"

"No, dear, that wasn't what I meant at all. I do like your dancing. If the circumstances were different, if I needed a new girl at my Club—but that's not it at all."

Loreen opened her mouth to babble some sort of apology, but the thought derailed somewhere along the vodka-marinated synapses between her brain and tongue, so that something altogether different slipped out. She heard herself ask, "Is it true you still strip?"

In the quiet room, it came out too forcefully. Then Daphne French smiled a smile that would have been almost maternal except for the eyes—the eyes rain-grey and cadaver cold—and Loreen felt the perfume and the vodka melting her down, turning her bones to warm aspic.

"Because my face looks old, you can't imagine I still dance. You think that's something you can only do when you're young. You wake up in the night and wonder what will it be like, whatever will you do, when the men don't look anymore."

Loreen said, "How did you—?" and Daphne French laughed.

"It ain't magic, honey. I don't need no crystal ball or Tarot cards to know that. But every pretty woman with a nice shape thinks that sooner or later, oh, Lordy, Lordy what will I do when the boys stop trippin' on their hard-ons chasin' after me. That's how I felt at your age. But I was different from most women. I never worried how I got what I wanted, s'long as I got it. It didn't hurt none either that I'd slept with everybody worth knowin' in New Orleans, so I had available to me some very valuable—connections.

"I wanted to stay young-lookin' enough to keep on dancing. Turned out it was just a matter of finding the right person—and working out a trade."

"But you're *not* young," Loreen said cautiously.

"No?"

To Loreen's astonishment, Daphne French removed her jacket and began unbuttoning her blouse. Beneath the thin silk, she wore nothing. Sedalia had not exaggerated. The woman's torso was unlined and smooth, the breasts beautifully pink-tipped, full and firm. Loreen found herself gaping like a schoolboy. In her work, she had seen a lot of boob jobs, but if this was one of them, the surgeon was a modern-day Michelangelo with silicon and a scalpel.

Revulsion and awe warred within her. The overall effect of Daphne French's appearance was harrowing, the weathered face and corrugated lids above the sleekly voluptuous torso.

"My God," breathed Loreen. "How did you—is it true then, the stories—?"

"Depends on what you've heard."

Daphne French gave a soft, gloating chuckle, reached into her evening bag and pulled out an ornate silver atomizer with a small, bejeweled bulb.

"But I'll tell you this, I never seduced no voodoo king or any of that garbage. My lover was a perfectly ordinary Catholic priest who'd made a life's career of exorcizing evil until I showed him what a fool he'd been and taught him to embrace it. He wanted me, and he was in a position to open certain doors that he found out might better have stayed shut. But I got what I wanted, a youthful-looking body and a means to stay this way. Now it's me that opens doors for people, honey, like my little priest once did for me. I show them how to find what they desire. You for instance. I know what you want."

As she spoke, Daphne French sprayed perfume on her breasts and neck, on the sleek, frosted dome of her hair.

To Loreen, it was like sinking into a floral sea, a suffocating olfactory brew of gardenias and musk. Almost gagging, she stared at the arabesque of light and color that seemed to undulate across Daphne French's skin.

"Take a good look, hon, and tell me what you see."

At first, Loreen's impression was that Daphne French's torso was covered with an elaborate tattoo and that some trick of the light created the illusion that the tattoos writhed. Or that the skin itself was moving, puckering and shifting the way a serpent's hide might ripple as the reptile glided through tall grass.

Then, peering closer, she made out figures, shapes, and drew back, violently repelled but helpless not to stare, like someone witnessing a particularly brutal mugging from the safety of a window high above.

Daphne French was not tattooed nor did her flesh creep with reptilian undulations, but something worse—a tableau of horror animated her upper body. It was as though the woman's torso were the entrance to a broad and terrible tunnel into which Loreen now gazed, toward which she was inexorably drawn.

She could see faces and limbs, parts of bodies interlaced and melded. The initial, overall effect reminded her of a photo she'd seen of sculptures in a Hindu temple, dozens of voluptuous women and wondrously endowed men, all intertwined and twisted, copulating in a skein of interwoven flesh.

Except, as Loreen looked, she realized this was, in fact, nothing like the coupling of the temple figures. These creatures engaged in acts of the most depraved self-mutilation, primitive and brutal matings with every kind of tool and blade.

Daphne French shifted her body so that new dimensions of the hellscape were revealed. Something different now, worse...

Loreen saw rows of cells, a tiered and looming prison, sensed the rhythmic pistoning of hands...

"Take it away!"

She drove her fists into her eyes. A hand heavy with rings touched her neck, caressing away the damp hair.

"Good girl. You did real fine. You looked longer than most do the first time."

Loreen pushed herself upright, away from that soft and violating voice. Her jaw was clenched so tightly that her teeth ached, and a clammy, sick-smelling sweat seeped from her pores.

"You put something in my drink."

69

"I don't need to drug people. You saw what you did because you wanted to."

Loreen didn't believe her. She'd played with PCP and mescaline a few times, and the sounds and colors they induced were nothing, a baby's crib toy, compared to this cornucopia of horrors.

"Get out of here. I don't know what you did to me, but go."

Daphne Fench uncurled herself from the couch with feral ease.

"I can imagine what you may have heard about me, hon, that I'm some kind of witchwoman, a devil worshipper, all kinds of tales—but one thing I bet nobody told you, and that's this: I never force nobody to do nothing. That's why I keep this hard old face. It's my badge of honor, my last vestige of integrity, if you will. I won't force people to do what they don't want to do. So you don't ever have to see that place again if that's your choice."

She scooped the ivory breasts back inside her blouse like a jeweler whisking diamonds into the display case, away from an unworthy customer, and looked at Loreen with amusement.

"I do know, hon. You want to find the one who killed your sister."

The brutal accuracy of the words iced Loreen's soul.

"Get out!" she shouted, wanting desperately to strike the woman but afraid to lay a hand on her.

At the door, Daphne French paused. "You call me, hon, if you get ready. There's more you haven't seen."

Sleep came with difficulty and, when it did, brought the nightmare that had tormented Loreen for years. Her older sister Allison, fourteen years old with a braid down her back and a throat livid with bruises, was peering in the window. Loreen tried to wake herself up, but it was like trying to swim through moist sand. Murky sleep dragged her down while the dream played itself out to its predictable, inevitable conclusion.

Allison went tap-tap, tap-tap on the glass. Behind her crowded a gang of boys, older boys from the 11th and 12th grades: Timmy Mercer and Ben Fitch and that awful bug-eyed Mack Strickland, who worked at the A & W Cafeteria and bragged about spitting in people's soup—or worse—if they pissed him off. All boys Loreen knew Allison had slept with, all crude and rough and hateful.

Tap-tap, went Allison again, and when Loreen looked, Allison twisted her mouth in that awful, soundless scream and hiked up her cheerleader skirt, the orange satin one she'd worn for the game with Dadeland High, now muddy and torn, blood streaked around the hem, caked on her legs.

"Go away!" screamed Loreen. "Go away or I'll tell Papa you screwed those boys for money."

Allison giggled merrily and flipped Loreen the bird. The fingernail was broken, blood pooling in the cuticle. She began to chant, in that raspy, strangled-out voice, "Careful, Loreen, be careful, careful, Loreen..."

And Loreen screaming, "Go to hell! I'm telling Papa on you!" and crying harder, because Papa had died, too, and it was all Allison's fault. After her body was found in a ditch off Alligator Alley, north of Ft. Lauderdale, he'd bought a gun and scraped together a reward, vowed to find his daughter's killer.

But after more than a year, the police gave up, and there weren't any real-life crime shows then to help the public track down criminals, so Papa got a little drunk one day, went out to the garage and performed fellatio on the barrel of his Colt .45.

After that, the burden of finding Allison's killer fell on Loreen.

"It's your fault Papa died," she shouted at her sister. "You stupid tramp, sleeping around town, your fault!"

She woke up in the pre-dawn purple, shaking from the dream, grateful at least that Larry wasn't there to see her sob. She made coffee, and was plucking away some dead leaves from her violets, when she smelled something and gasped like someone accidentally fingering a small and venomous snake. Between two flowerpots in the windowsill sat the silver atomizer.

In the chilly dawn, a new fragrance, earthy, invigorating, emanated from the bottle. She touched it and the scent at once transferred to her skin. She whiffed her fingertips, aroused by the subtle delicacy of the odor.

"*Don't*," some part of her mind pleaded, but she gave the bulb a tiny pinch. Sweet dew streamed out onto her wrist.

The scent was different this morning. Roses and honey. A light, clean scent, sweet enough to drink. She sprayed her throat. The odor swelled. A dab between her breasts, her thighs. Her head bloomed with flowers, a dizzying engulfment of roses, honey and roses, roses and—blood.

She sat down—or tried to, but found that she was already horizontal, splayed out on the floor, looking down at her flat, naked belly. Her navel oozed with colors, a spiraling mandala. She felt herself sucked down into the moving tapestry. The colors darkened. The perfume went rancid, foul. Like bleak cliffs, the howling cages loomed, and she was...

...dancing. Oiled and naked, her muscled body sheened with light. The cages, long and desolate rows, hung suspended from glassine cords. Loreen undulated across a mirrored stage, seeing every detail of the captives with preternatural vision.

The men were naked. Hideously aroused. Fists thrust madly up and down. A field of angry red batons, swollen to the point the bruised and purple meat must surely split, burst open at the bulb like rotted fruit.

Up, down, up down, updownupdownupdown...

At the base of each man's member were fastened metal rings. Loreen realized what she had at first taken for sexual arousal was really a brutally maintained engorgement.

The masturbators howled and cursed. Bands of putrid flesh ringed the metal, and from the purple, enflamed heads dribbled tiny beads of blood.

Appalled yet fascinated, Loreen danced from cage to cage. Who were these men and what could they have done to merit such atrocities?

At once, as though the mere thinking of the question tapped some source of knowledge beyond herself, the answers came: Here pumped and grunted Henry Beddington, a balding, hawk-nosed dentist who'd buggered homeless men in 1930's London, sliced out their tongues to still their cries and—

Bobby Darryl Keene, who ran the ferris wheel and raped teenage girls on Cony Island and—

Bledsoe Cheever, who tortured prostitutes in Detroit and Madison throughout the 1960's and—

Jaime Ramirez, who kept his victims trussed and gagged beneath his bed...

The cages seemed to stretch into infinity, the farthest occupants in shadow, and Loreen felt compelled to see the next face and the next, and she knew that she could dance forever, into hell itself, and hadn't she done just that, to perform before this foul and shrieking horde.

She wet a finger, touched herself, and breathed her own aroma as it mingled with the overpowering odor of the men's' arousal.

One more cage, one more…

Did you know Allison?

But the dream, the hallucination, whatever it was, was fading out. The nightmare cracked like a dropped egg as Loreen sat up on her kitchen floor, clinging to the tile as though afraid it would tilt out from under her, and watched dully as a cockroach carried off a bread crumb from beneath the sink.

Her body smelled of something vile. She rushed to the bathroom, clung to the toilet like a life preserver while she heaved herself dry, then dragged her quivering body into the shower.

The phone rang while she was bathing. Got quiet, rang some more. Who would call this early? Finally, wrapped in a towel, she staggered from the bathroom and snatched it up.

A sigh of disgust. Larry's. "Why aren't you here?"

He was angry, but why? She was the one who should be mad, him calling at this hour.

"Where am I supposed to be at—" And then the thought came, even as he said it, "Tujaque's. You were supposed to meet me for lunch at one."

"But it's not even seven—" She saw the wall clock then, well into afternoon.

"I overslept, okay? Do you have to make a big deal of it?"

"Yes, I guess I do. I was worried when you stood me up."

She hated the direction this was taking, his goodness, her guilt.

"Look, I can't talk right now."

His voice changed. "Is someone with you?"

"That's right. You've got it. One of my many lovers." She made her voice breathy, low. "Harder, darling, harder."

"Loreen, enough. I don't think I deserve this kind of treatment. We need to talk."

She thought, he's breaking up with me, this is it, and said, "All right. When?" Flat and harsh, like she was responding to a summons into traffic court, and she felt no fear or sadness, only a strange longing and a terrible compulsion to look into more of the cages.

She met Larry that night in the dining room of the Fairmont, where candles flickered softly and a toffee-colored singer crooned from a blue-lit platform. The platform and lights made Loreen think of the cages and her appetite departed, leaving her to pick idly at her steak while Larry wolfed down his lobster thermador with gusto enough for both of them.

She knew he ate heartiest when ill at ease, a knowledge that increased her conviction that this was break-up time. What was the old advice? Always take them to a posh spot so they couldn't make a scene when you dropped the bomb.

"...and I've made up my mind. I can't see any other way," Larry was saying. "I want us to get married."

The morsel of steak Loreen was chewing went down the wrong way. She thought "Heimlich Maneuver" and grabbed her water glass, and when she finally had her breath again, she laughed.

"You can't be that surprised. You knew I was working up to it."

"I guess after I missed our lunch—I lied, you know. No one was with me when you called. I just wanted to hurt you."

"I know. But, why? What have I done?"

"Nothing. You're fine. It's me, it's always me."

"So, what's your answer?"

"Jesus."

"Is that a prayer or a curse?"

"Both."

"One thing, though." He stopped eating and used his fork for emphasis, tap-tap on the tablecloth. "I want you to give up dancing. Wait, don't answer yet. Just listen. I don't want to make a demand like this, a request, that is, based on some kind of male ego problem. But I don't think I'm being unreasonable. The idea of you up there naked, of men gawking at you—I can't deal with it anymore."

"Larry, that's how you *met* me. Gawking."

She knew how he hated being reminded of that, that he liked to pretend coming into the Casbah after work had been a one-time aberration—he was sleep-walking, hypnotized, held at gunpoint.

"Loreen, this can be worked out. I love you."

He was tapping the fork faster now, and she wanted to hit him with her fist, but she used words instead. "How can I believe you love me? My own father didn't even love me enough to stay alive after my sister - "

But she stopped short, because suddenly she smelled a stunning odor, the most intensely carnal scent she could imagine—the heady, pungent odor of a room where a prostitute brings her johns, of used dildos and sheets sticky with sweat and saliva and cum—and Loreen saw Daphne French leaving the dining room, her snowy hair twisted into a Gordian knot, white and shiny as the tip of a glacier.

"What's wrong?" Larry said.

Loreen rose from her chair, but a group of women wearing convention buttons was coming into the dining room and she lost sight of Daphne French. "That woman who just left."

Larry blinked. "Where?"

"She's gone now. But that odor. Don't tell me you don't *smell* that."

He gaped at her, mouth duplicating that of the mackerel on a passing platter.

"The appetizer?" he said finally. "Was something wrong with the snails?"

Her plants were dead. Whole rows of them in the windowsills, desiccated and brown.

The atomizer's perfume had changed again. A new fragrance, musky and dark, like an Asian love potion, wafted up from the bottle. Loreen breathed its opium fragrance, anointed it onto her belly and neck.

She undressed and lay across the bed. The walls and ceiling shimmied. What felt like a bouquet of serpents writhed behind her forhead. Beneath her eyelids strobed an afterimage of Daphne French's torso, the breasts full and round like crimson goblets, the belly plugged by what Loreen first took to be an enormous ruby, until she realized that the navel formed a bloody entranceway, a flaming hole like an inverted umbilical cord into Daphne French's corrupt heart.

Loreen shut her eyes and gripped the mattress as the bed began to drop. Her cheek struck something hard, teeth scraping splintery floorboards.

When she opened her eyes the cages ringed her, men yelling, moaning. Loreen lifted her arms above her head. Her hands floated off in the air and then returned to her wrists like circling doves. The miracle seemed unimportant. Trivial. She undulated between the rows, plucking at her hardened nipples, massaging the delta of pubic hair. The men, jerked raw, hissed at her. Warm spit pelted her face, pearled in her hair.

Loreen caressed herself in rhythm with the men.

"*Go back*," implored the small part of her mind that was still sane, but at every corner, another corridor opened up, and she had to look inside those cages, too, it was important, there was still time to go back, still time... *did you know Allison?*

When Loreen didn't answer her phone for several days, Larry used his key to enter the apartment.

He found her curled up on the bedroom floor, her fingernails clawed away, tongue chewed to pulp. A foul-smelling, sick-sweet odor clung to her body, like food gone rancid.

Her body, when he gathered it up, was supple still, the flesh not yet cold. For an instant, he thought he saw a flickering behind her lids, colors and subtle patterns, like geometries of light reflected off very pale water. Then the illusion of movement, of life still clung to, vanished, and Larry looked into her agate eyes and saw they were hard and dead as glass.

Loreen heard something slam—her heart?—in the far distance of the corridors. Daphne French's laughter, like soiled velvet, was a soft and sibilant caress inside her mind.

"I knew you'd dance for me in Hell. That's why I chose you. I knew you loved a monster."

The voice and Loreen's heartbeat both faded into silence.

Loreen knew there was no going back now, ever, but the loss seemed minor, unremarkable.

Up and down the rows of men she danced, up down, up down, updownupdownupdown…

…searching for the worst of all, the murderers of children, heard the door shut on her own cage, and saw inside the man she sought, who waited for her.

Finally.

Papa.

KNOCKOUTS

It was the sea that brought him the first one.

Charlie had been awake most of the night, tossing and turning and beating his meat in his one uncooled room. Finally he could stand his state of sweaty arousal no longer. Pulling on a pair of shorts and a tropical shirt, he went outside. The beach was on the other side of A1-A, a few hundred yards via a plank walkway through tall marsh grass. He could hear the muted suck and thunder of the waves as he approached it.

The night was sultry, moist, heavy with heat and the soft, throbbing whir of insects. He stepped off the planking onto powdery brown sand just as the first tendrils of pink touched the horizon like a faint lipstick smear.

He was looking at that pink smear or he wouldn't have seen her, the lone swimmer, her flailing arm a dark bar briefly bisecting the light. He took a few steps toward the sea. By that time he could hear her screams.

Charlie stripped his shirt off, took a few running steps through the surf, and hurled himself into the ocean.

The next few minutes were still a black blur to him. He wasn't that strong a swimmer, having grown up in rural Indiana and moved to Florida only the year before, scrounging for manual labor jobs in the wake of Hurricane Andrew. The tide was high, the sea hungry, eager for the chance to drink down two victims instead of one.

Cold and frightened, already swallowing brine, Charlie wanted to turn back. But a part of his mind, the stern, angry, whip-wielding part, wouldn't allow him to falter. A woman was in danger. Charlie's mother had brought him up to think of women as special, sacred, superior in every way to men, who were filthy-minded and only wanted one thing. Women were to be placed upon a pedestal, protected, cherished. A real man would risk his life for one in danger.

So Charlie floundered on.

He had lost sight of her, was treading water in the trough of a wave, when suddenly she skidded down the side of an oncoming wall of water like a bodysurfer out of control. She crashed into Charlie and wrapped her arms around him in a death grip. She was a small woman, but panic made her fiercely strong. She was climbing up onto Charlie's shoulders, forcing him under water.

Charlie struggled to keep his head above the surface. A wave lifted and flung them. Charlie looked into the woman's terror-stricken eyes and felt his dick get stiff. He made a fist and drove it hard into the woman's jaw. Her eyes rolled back.

He swung an arm around her neck and started breast-stroking toward shore.

The beach was still deserted when Charlie reached it.

He picked the woman up, chuckling to himself as he got a mental image of King Kong lifting Fay Ray, carried her up the bank into the tall marsh grass and laid her on the ground.

In the dark, Charlie couldn't see her well. He liked that. It meant she didn't have a face, not really, she didn't even exist. She was a secret between him and the ocean.

He stepped out of his shorts.

Always respect a woman, his mother used to say.

Yanked the woman's sopping tank suit down over her ankles.

Put her on a pedestal. Treat her like a queen.

Rammed his dick inside her, sand, sea water, and all. It hurt but Charlie was too excited to care. He fucked and fucked, and he wanted so bad to come, he was dying to come, but he couldn't, he…just…couldn't…, and about that time the woman moaned and started to come around, so he slugged her again, and she sagged back onto the sand with a little trickle of blood coming out of her mouth.

Put a woman on a pedestal, treat her like gold, keep those nasty-boy ideas out of your head.

He thrust in sweaty, grunting desperation, like a man trying to dig a grave with his cock, but he still couldn't come—he could *never* come—and it made him furious, so he waited until the woman started to come to and then he punched her again…and again and again…until he came with a roar that he muffled by biting into the flesh of her tit, but there was no pleasure in it, he felt like his balls were being pulled out the hole in his cock, and his cheeks were soaked with tears of rage and disgust that he had let his mother down.

But he was done. Finally.

For now.

Sore and exhausted, Charlie retrieved his clothes. The sun had just risen over the edge of the horizon like a buttered bun in a pop-up toaster. He squinted down at the woman. There wasn't a lot of her face left, but she was still breathing. Charlie walked down to the edge of the ocean and washed the blood off his knuckles.

He went home and dressed for work and spent the day pushing wheelbarrowfuls of cement around the construction site of a motel that was being rebuilt after being flattened by Andrew. His dick didn't give him much trouble, even when a couple of schoolgirls flounced by, giggling and giving the workmen the eye, and he didn't think of the drowned woman again until the next day when the *Miami Herald* carried a headline about the brutal rape-murder of a Wyoming tourist named Deborah Engels visiting Miami for a nursing convention.

That one, the first one, was for free. That was the one the sea gave him.

After that, Charlie kept trying to achieve satisfaction the way he usually did. Alone, in the privacy of his torrid little room, he would beat his seven inches til the crown purpled and bled, and he thought about Deborah Engels and about the pleasure that had shot hand-to-groin when his fist slammed into her face, but he still didn't come. He bought over-priced magazines wrapped in cellophane with names like *Buxum Bondagettes* and *Babes in Torment* and fantasized about what he'd like to do to them, but his dick remained recalcitrant, like a gun you could cock but not fire. (Because women belonged on pedestals, after all, Mama had said, and no nasty man should even want to put his hands on them—let alone shoot jism all over their pictures.)

On those infrequent occasions when she'd caught him masturbating as a boy, Mama had used a leather riding crop to reinforce the notion that God intended dicks for peeing only and male minds should be kept as white and clean as a freshly scrubbed-out, never shat in, toilet.

Yet even now, despite the bad memories, Charlie kept a photo of his mother on the table by the bed: hatted for church, sultry as a

Florida August in her faux pearls and heavy make-up. Looking like a whore and acting like a saint as she wagged her cutie-pie ass up to the rail to take communion from a minister who peeked down her cleavage as he slid the wafer onto her tongue.

Sometimes, in desperation, Charlie turned his mother's picture to the wall, although he felt guilty doing so; at other times he stared at it as though hypnotized. Next to the photo, he kept another fetish object, an agate statuette of a buxum, naked woman on an inch-high pedestal. Charlie had won the paperweight throwing balls through wooden hoops at a carnival back in Indiana when he was only twelve. For years it had stayed hidden at the back of his closet. Now, far from Mama's prying eyes, he could admire this trophy salvaged from a wretched adolescence during which whippings with the riding crop were as much a part of the weekly routine as the trek to church. Charlie liked to look at the woman's mottled agate breasts, her stone cooze shot through with vermillion, and remember his mother's favorite saying about how women should be put on pedestals. Charlie thought that this was the only kind of pedestal women belonged on, posing nude for a man's pleasure like some kind of circus animal. It made him feel more powerful to think such thoughts, more in control, but, lately, it didn't help him climax.

Before he pulled the woman from the sea, Charlie had been able to come, if not regularly or reliably, then at least often enough so as not to feel half crazy with frustration. But after the morning on the beach with Deborah Engels, it was as if his mother's voice in Charlie's head got nastier, meaner. It interrupted his lushest fantasies with cries of *Pervert!*

Degenerate!; it stopped him on the verge of shooting off a wad so many times he finally wept with longing and wanted to bang his head into the wall until he slumped unconscious. It was as if his mother were there in the room with him, as if she leaned over his humid bed and shrieked while he frictioned himself raw.

He was growing desperate, thinking about ways to hurt himself, wondering if pain might be enough to make him come, when he made the decision not to wait for another gift from the sea, but to take the next one himself.

《《—》》

Her name was Peggy Ingersoll. In her late twenties, she was already spent-looking. Nicotine had scraped all melodiousness from her voice; alcohol had left her jowly and bloated, with a case of the shakes if you encountered her before her first shot of the morning.

Charlie would sit next to her at the Seabreeze Bar after work, downing rail drinks and occasionally, when he was feeling flush, buying a few for Peggy. That was enough to cinch their friendship; the mere scent of gin made her purr like a stroked alleycat. For a fifth slipped into her purse, she'd meet Charlie out back of the Seabreeze and take his cock in her red-lipsticked mouth or into the cleft of her tattooed tits. Though her sucking was lusty, almost frantic, as if she were performing mouth-to-dick resuscitation, Charlie would get just to the point of climax and then bog down. He just couldn't let go.

And Peggy always looked defeated, like his failure to spurt was somehow a black mark on what must otherwise have been a pristine cocksucking record.

"It ain't your fault, babe," Charlie told her. "I prob'ly had a might too much to drink is all."

Peggy shrugged, still doing her imitation of a Hoover. "Usually too much booze just makes 'em limp. You're hard as a cop's nightstick, honey."

He didn't want to hit Peggy. He really didn't. She looked like life had roughed her up enough, with sixty years of hard times in her thirty-year-old alkie eyes and a booze gut that made her look like she had a bun half-way to done in her oven.

He didn't want to hurt her, but then he saw her one night, heading from her daytime job at a Hialeah Hojo's up A1-A toward the Seabreeze. By that time, Charlie was going into his fiftieth hour of arousal-induced sleep deprivation, and his cock was abraded from his desperate efforts to get release.

Charlie was driving his '81 Chrysler, headed for the Seabreeze himself. He swung up to the curb. Peggy got in without a word, like she'd been expecting him to drive by and pick her up. Her expression, dull-eyed, defeated, told Charlie all he needed to know: she was already brutalized by life, he could hardly do worse by her.

He didn't take her to the Seabreeze, of course, but along a dirt road heading toward the beach, after stopping for a six-pack at a convenience store.

The dark enfolded them like protective wings. Love bugs, locked in airborne copulation, buzzed in buggy lewdness around their heads.

Charlie suggested a stroll up the beach. Peggy was on her third Bud already. She grabbed a fourth for the road, and they meandered up the dark beach, the sea seething at their ankles, beer rumbling in their guts.

When they stopped next to a darkened dune, Peggy drained the last of the beer and dropped with a grunt to her knees, fumbling for Charlie's zipper. He let her take him out and into her mouth, all sloppy with beery saliva.

When she had him thoroughly lubricated, Charlie lifted her to her feet.

"Let's do somethin' different tonight, honey."

He'd figured a straight fuck ought to be no problem. But she surprised him by flat out refusing.

"I don't do that," she said. "I do hand and I do mouth, but no pussy. I don't do pussy."

"Why not?"

"Are you crazy? I don't want to get AIDS."

"I got rubbers."

"They break."

But he'd made up his mind. He had to come. If he waited one minute longer, his brains were going to explode out the end of his dick like so much white cheese.

"I'm sorry, honey," he said and swung a mean right into Peggy's jaw. She went down, but there was still fight in her.

She rolled to the side and tried to scurry away. Charlie grabbed a fistful of hair and twisted her around, popped her in the chin til she folded, then threw her back, kicked her legs apart, and released his dick, which bounced forth like a cage-crazy hound while he tore off her panties and mounted her.

For long minutes he lay there, thrusting himself into her unresistant form, bruising the head of his dick and bruising her face, and every time he hit her, his dick would strain and stiffen until it felt like the blood vessels along the shaft were going to pop like overstretched hemorrhoids, but the voice was ranting in his head, as Mama of the Whip intoned, *You put a woman on a pedestal, respect her. You never, ever hit a woman,* and every time the voice said that, Charlie battered Peggy's face, but he didn't come and after twenty or so minutes, his erection died away of sheer exhaustion, and Peggy just plain died.

«« — »»

The experience with Peggy was so unsatisfactory that for a few weeks Charlie didn't even try to jerk off. He stopped buying *Buxum Bondagettes* and the rest of the s/m rags and got reeling drunk every night, so smashed that his cock couldn't have gotten up even if ten naked babes in bondage had squirmed hog-tied across the floor of his bedroom.

Then one night some of the guys on the construction job were going to a place called Pure Platinum, a pussy palace near Coconut Grove, famed for a bevy of blondes whom the wonders of diet and cosmetic surgery had endowed with wasp waists and Barbie-doll boobs and the wheat hair of lushly-maned ponies. Pure Platinum was known for some mildly kinky extras, like naked trapeze acts and Jell-O wrestling contests. Tonight, when Charlie and his buddies drove up, the sign on the marquee read: *Knock-outs: All Girl Boxing, 10 pm.*

"Hey, what the fuck," Charlie said, "do they actually hit each other?"

"Naw, it's all fake," said Cleeg, a scrawny dude from west Texas with a goiter the size of a golf ball twanging in his neck. "They just poof around at each other with them little gloves. Don't wanna mess up them pretty faces or put a dent in them silicone tits."

Put a woman on a pedestal, treat her like a queen.

Charlie's dick, although already tranquilized with half a dozen bourbons, began to stir.

"C'mon," said Cleeg, "let's watch them bitches fight."

As it turned out, Cleeg was right about the quality of the boxing: the fights were stagey and silly, more like sorority girls boffing each other with pillows than anything approximating real boxing. Their one redeeming value was that the girls performed topless, melonous mammaries bouncing in sweet parody of their gloved hands. Toward the end, though, there was a girl named Roxane, tall and long-limbed with a thoroughbred ass and the kind of sleekly packed biceps that suggested significant time spent in weight rooms; she boxed with an energy that went beyond show, delivering a few well-placed, if pulled punches, that left her opponant's face splotchy red.

"Wow," Cleeg said, "what a knock-out she is," and for a second Charlie gaped at him, thinking Cleeg had said something outrageously filthy, even for Cleeg. Then he realized Cleeg just meant the girl was pretty.

"Yeah, I wouldn't mind getting into those boxing trunks."

"In your dreams," said Cleeg, "in your dreams."

«« — »»

In his dreams. She walked into an uppercut that imbedded her lower teeth in the roof of her mouth like stalactites while her legs, like the gates to Paradise, swung wide before him, and he poured himself into her, coming and coming while the unspilled seed of a thousand fruitless mastabatory sessions gushed from his dick in milky torrents, and he woke up moaning, rutting wildly into the mattress, but the voice in his head screamed *Nasty!*, *Filthy!* and the hole in the head of his penis might as well have been plugged with cement.

He woke up with his face twisted toward the nightstand, where Mama of the Whip and the Naked Lady on the Pedestal eyed his pitiful efforts at self-pleasuring with cold disdain.

Never hit a woman. Put her on a pedestal. Treat her like a queen.

Charlie hadn't come since the morning on the beach with Deborah Engels almost two months earlier. Peggy had been a disaster, but maybe that was because the booze had already done a number on her face and body even before Charlie's fists got into the act. Charlie decided he needed someone sexier. He needed Roxane, topless and slick with sweat in her red satin boxing trunks.

So he began to plan it.

At first he thought of grabbing Roxane when she left Pure Platinum, but that was no good, because a bouncer walked the girls to their cars. Nobody came to meet the girls when they arrived, however, and Charlie soon learned that Roxane didn't get to work until 9:30 pm.

When she arrived at the club a few nights later, Charlie was parked nearby. Roxane got out of her Datsun wearing jeans and a black sweatshirt with the logo of a local gym on the front, carrying a tote bag that must have contained her costume. Charlie ambled over and asked if she'd autograph a picture he'd taken of her for a buddy. She looked Charlie over like he was week-old bread and said she was in a hurry. Charlie showed her a twenty, which she palmed with greed almost as naked as her body had been in the skimpy boxing trunks.

"Here, let me get the picture," said Charlie, lifting the trunk of his car. As it opened, Roxane took a step backward.

Charlie yanked her forward by the hair. Before she could scream, he punched her in the side of the head—one, two—fast and hard, threw her sideways into the trunk, tossed her tote bag in on top of her, roped her hands behind her and slammed the trunk shut.

He got behind the wheel. In all, the subduing and abduction of Roxane had taken less than twenty seconds.

Charlie drove back to his efficiency on A1-A, careful to stay just below the speed limit and come to a full stop at all red lights.

At home, he parked so the trunk was only a few feet from the front door, slung Roxane over his shoulder, and carried her inside—an exposure time he figured was less than ten seconds and was virtually invisible in the ill-lit rental complex.

Inside he threw Roxane across the bed, stripped off her jeans and underpants and his own and climbed aboard the buttery expanse of her torso. He debated whether or not to tape her mouth, but decided that, if she got noisy, he could shut her up quickly enough.

With the first thrust into her perfumed pussy, Charlie got a surprise. Unlike Deborah Engels and Peggy, who'd been so dry that fucking them was like jerking off into sandpaper, Roxane was moist and hot, like fucking the inside of a buttered biscuit.

As he worked, she moaned and rolled her head luxuriantly from side to side. A spectacular bruise was flowering on her jaw, but her lips were curved into a smile approaching radiance.

"Oh, God," she said. "I came. I came so hard I think I died."

Charlie stopped thrusting.

"You mean…just now?"

"When you hit me, I came like crazy." Wickedness flashed in her blue eyes, as she added, "That's the best orgasm there is, but most men are too chickenshit to hit me hard enough."

"But that ain't possible. I knocked you cold."

"And made me come. Right at that second. It's like an incredible explosion…the blow and the orgasm combined. It's the only way I can come. It's why I started doing the boxing show at the club. I thought…I guess it's silly but…I thought there might be other girls like me and I might meet them. But it didn't turn out like that. Everyone's so scared of getting hurt or hurting someone else that they don't hit hard at all.

"But you knew what I like, and you don't even know me. How is that?"

The urge to punch her again warred in Charlie with the desire to hear more. Just the fact that she was talking to him, not struggling or begging to be set free, threw his plans off balance.

"I have trouble coming myself," he heard himself say. "It's like I can't let go. Unless I hurt somebody and lately…"

She looked up, apparently unafraid. "Yes?"

"…not even then. Even when I…when I was hurting somebody, the last time I still couldn't get off."

"I'll bet I could make you come."

As she said it, Charlie's eyes went almost involuntarily to the picture of his mother, the agate paperweight of the woman on the pedestal.

Put a woman on a pedestal, treat her like gold.

A surge of hormones and sadism pumped the blood into his hard-on until it felt like the jawbone of a whale.

"Don't need any help," he said, ramming into her pussy with all his weight as he brought his fist around into her cheek. A red welt blossomed under one eye. She sighed and didn't move again for a while, but her cunt stayed just as succulently juicy as before and the blissful look upon her face implied more a contented sleep than unconsciousness.

Charlie fucked her until she came around, but he didn't hit her again. Instead he asked her if she had really gotten off.

"Incredibly. Like rockets." Her breath was coming in little breathy gasps. "My God, I know I'm getting beaten up, but these orgasms are to die for."

Charlie considered this. His cock was a rod of fire, his hips ached from thrusting, and his balls felt like bags of concrete, but as near as he could tell, he was no closer to coming than when he'd started.

"You said you could help me get off. How?"

"You know how. By hitting you, of course. You'd have to let me punch you."

"Aw, come on. You ain't that strong. You couldn't knock me out."

"I wouldn't have to. Just one punch, just so you could let go. That's all it would take. You'd come like you'd never believe."

Roxane's left eye was swelling shut. A trail of blood had meandered from her lower lip and dried along her cheek. She didn't look so foxy anymore, not like anybody you'd want to put up on a pedestal, Charlie thought, but perversely, the worse she looked, the more painfully hard became his boner.

"All right, get up."

She did so, but she was wobbly. When Charlie untied her wrists, she teetered forward, knocking the items on the nightstand, the photo and the paperweight and a stack of *Buxum Bondagettes* to the floor.

"I need my tote bag."

Charlie tossed it to her. She sat on the floor amid the spilled magazines, the bruises on her face contrasting with the ripe, tawny flesh of her body, and began to root around inside the bag.

It occurred to Charlie she might have a gun or a can of Mace in there.

"Hey, I need to see your hands. What've you got in there?"

By way of answer, she threw him one of her boxing gloves. Charlie tossed it up and down a few times, imagining it was her boob, severed from her body but still bouncy, firm. He put the idea away for possible use later on.

When he looked back, she was scrambling around on the floor, hurriedly lacing the other glove onto her right hand. "I need to wear the glove, otherwise when I hit you, I could break my hand."

That brought a grin to Charlie's face—like she thought a broken hand was going to matter when this was over.

"Now hold onto your dick," Roxane said, "and get ready to shoot to the ceiling. If you don't start to come like gangbusters when I pop you, I won't know why not."

Charlie spit into his hand, stroked his stiff rod.

"One punch," he said. "One punch is all you get, and if I don't come just the way you say, then it's my turn, and I'll hurt you, I'll hurt you bad."

"One punch is all I need," she said, and something that felt a lot harder than any fist slammed into the side of Charlie's mouth. His eyes flew open, and she slugged him again, a brutal uppercut that rocked back his head. This time he swayed and flopped onto the bed, arms up to fend her off, but she was on top of him and the thing she'd put inside the glove before she laced it up—stone, a heavy slab of stone, shaped like the bottom of a pedestal, the kind you were supposed to put a woman on—shattered his jaw in two places, and the next blow cracked his cheekbone and the one after that smeared the cartilage of his nose in a ruby stripe across his cheek and...

...somewhere, far off, beyond the firestorm of pain in his smashed face, he heard Roxane cry out that she was coming.

She had lied to him, though. Not just about hitting him only one time, but about something else, too. It was the last thing in this life that Charlie learned. Because it wasn't at the moment of unconsciousness that he climaxed, but much later, at the point of death, that he came and came.

FEAR OF PHOBIAS

Paul Twitchell stared down at the hands that had cracked Tom McGee's neck like a Thanksgiving wishbone and tried desperately to stop them from shaking. Glancing over to see if Olsun, the guard, was watching, he snatched up a magazine and pretended to read. Killer or not, if he couldn't get his hands under control, the shrink would think he was some kind of wuss.

Dr. Davenport's waiting room, on the fifth floor of Mobley Psychiatric Center in Dallas, was tastefully decorated with deep brown leather sofas, hunting prints and antique pistols. No chrome or glass here. Except for the stacks of dog-eared *Psychology Today*'s, it looked like a rich Englishman's study.

Not so bad hanging out in a place like this a couple of times a week, thought Twitchell, not after an eight by ten cell with the crapper in the corner and the walls bedecked with his cellmate's cum-encrusted "Chubby Chicks" pin-ups, whose mountainous flesh could put a normal guy off sex forever. Twitchell hated shrinks, despised the smug, condescending bastards, but at least getting out of his cell for few hours in order to be studied was—

Christ, what the hell was that!

The shriek was muffled and emanated from somewhere farther back in the office complex, but its primal terror blanked Twitchell's mind as if an earthquake had canted the building. His fingers dug into the armrest of his chair like a man being rocketed to Mars. He looked at Olsun, who shrugged mile-wide shoulders and smirked as though the sight of Twitchell's terror gave him a hard-on.

"Scared? A tough guy like you?"

"I hate shrinks," said Twitchell, although what he wanted was to ask who would scream like that and what had been done to them to produce such a sound.

"Wanna back out now, big man?" taunted Olsun, whose I.Q., Twitchell figured, hovered somewhere around his shirt size.

The scream came again. Several screams actually, but run

together in such acute panic that they fused into a demented yip-ping, like a coyote on PCP.

"What the fuck *is* that?"

"Just some guy gettin' butt-fucked with a Phillips screwdriver, I reckon, said Olsun amiably, "or maybe they're fryin' his nuts with electroshock." He smiled down at Twitchell, his full lips like slugs copulating in the raw slab of a face. "You wanna back out now?"

Oh, desperately so! The idea of accruing gain time in return for a few sessions with Dallas' well-known phobia specialist had seemed like a good deal when it was proposed to him. Now Twitchell was thinking he might have screwed up royally.

But as much as the screams made his balls shrivel and his gut roil like a small boat in a cyclone, Olsun's shit-eating grin was less bearable.

"Fuck it," said Twitchell. "I don't have nothin' to worry about. I got rights. The doc, he can't do nothin' less I give my permission."

Another scream, hyphenated with short hiccupy grunts. Was it a woman screaming or a man? Twitchell couldn't tell and that scared him most of all. The magazine began to rattle in his hands.

Olsun laughed down from his six foot plus height, his weightlifter biceps swollen like engorged pythons under his puke-colored uniform.

Twitchell was wondering how many of those tobacco-stained teeth he could rearrange with the one punch he might get in before Olsun floored him, when a bosomy black nurse with a Jamaican accent called out his name.

Olsun accompanied him into Davenport's office. After shaking hands and offering coffee (which Twitchell declined, bad for the nerves), Davenport told Olsun to wait outside. There was a TV monitor where he could keep an eye on his charge from the nurses' station. Twitchell wondered if this was standard practice or if, having met him, the burly doctor felt a man of Twitchell's diminu-tive stature couldn't possibly pose any threat.

Even without his credentials as a psychiatrist, author, and lec-turer, Breck Davenport would have been intimidating. His height, almost equal to Olsun's, and jutting Marlboro-man jaw made Twitchell feel insectile, runty, undersized—an instant reason for him to loathe the man. Women were always bitching about pussy-discrimination, but didn't anybody realize the enormous, unrelenting cruelties that were perpetrated on smaller males, those whose height and weight and musculature (not to mention genital-size) made them less than brute-looking?

God, how he hated being puny and how he'd tried to make up for it—by picking fights and studying *tae kwon do,* by teeth-gritting it through macho jobs like the one on the loading dock where he'd killed McGee. All his life Twitchell had been goaded, laughed at, bullied and teased by males whose genetic inheritance had given them Hulk Hogan physiques and Bluto brains.

And his name—that didn't help any.

At the loading dock, he was known as Twitchy-Pie or Twitchy-Toes. Those were some of the milder ones. And when his phobia became known—when McGee started calling him "Miss Twitchy"—that had sent him over the fucking edge.

So what if he'd attacked the bastard from behind. The Neanderthal never knew what hit him when Twitchell's elbow caught him at the juncture between skull and spine, shattering vertebrae. It was almost worth a murder rap to know he'd gotten the better of a much larger, stronger man.

Davenport took a seat and said affably, "You're trembling, Mr. Twitchell. Please relax. We're here to do a simple interview. Don't be afraid."

"It's a hereditary thing," said Twitchell. "Got nothin' to do with fear."

"I see. Well, I understand you claim to get a severe phobic reaction in certain situations, but I need something more specific. Could you elaborate?"

"No."

"Why not?"

"It's personal."

"Yes, well—" Davenport's smile looked sprayed on, "—if I'm going to help you, I have to know which phobia you suffer from."

"I thought the idea was to study me. I don't need no *help.*"

"Look, Mr. Twitchell, the understanding was you'd get gain time off your sentence if you did this interview. So let's get on with it."

Twitchell shrugged, a gesture he intended to appear disdainful, but which turned into a humiliating shudder as sounds from across the hall reached him. Someone—a man, Twitchell was sure of it—was weeping softly, defeatedly, the soft sobs of the broken and wretched. What made it even worse was that Twitchell was positive this person was not the same one who had been screaming earlier.

Davenport tapped his pen sharply on the desk.

"Are you afraid of enclosed spaces?"

"No."

"Heights?"

"Hell, no, why way back before they was doin' them bungee jumps, I used to—"

"Water?"

"Swim like a fuckin' duck."

"Cats? Dogs? Lizards?"

Twitchell shook his head. "Look, doc, I thought we was gonna talk about me in general. My family history, y'know, do I hate my Mom, how often do I jerk off, maybe look at some inkblots, that kinda thing. Stuff the shrinks done with me before."

"Agoraphobic?"

"Y'know, it really pisses me off, doc, when you won't talk English. I didn't go to college, O.K.? That make me lessa man?"

"Of course not. I never implied—Mr. Twitchell, you're shaking again."

"It's them goddamn noises," yelled Twitchell. "One's screamin', one's cryin', what the fuck's goin' on? Man can't hear himself think."

Davenport sighed. "You're here on a busy morning. It *is* noisy. And I can appreciate how upsetting it must be when you don't know the cause of the sounds." Davenport pushed aside his notebook and pen. "Let me give you a tour. That way you'll see there's nothing sinister going on here."

"Olsun don't gotta tag along, does he?"

Davenport seemed to consider this. Twitchell guessed the good doctor, who was built like your basic Frigidaire, was sizing him up and probably thinking something along the lines of, *I could squash this little twerp like a mosquito.* Well, McGee had thought that, too—once.

"No, Mr. Twitchell, I see no need for a guard. We'll take a look around, and if you decide you don't want to be a part of my study, that's up to you."

They proceeded past two open doorways. Twitchell glimpsed an office with what appeared to be records and a nurses' station full of monitoring equipment.

"We'll start with something simple," said Davenport. Opening a door on the right, he motioned for Twitchell to proceed. He did, and but for clamping down on his tongue, nearly let loose a shriek of fright.

Below yawned a gaping chasm. Of course, Twitchell knew that couldn't be the case, because he was obviously standing on something. Below—far below—termite-sized cars crawled along labarinthean boulevards, people the size of fleas scurried along sidewalks. As Twitchell slowly realized the images were being projected onto a solid floor, he grew more confident and stepped out into the room, but the illusion was still unnerving.

"I'm rather proud of this room. It's my own invention," Davenport said. "Acrophobics, people with a fear of heights, spend time in here. Ideally, one would be able to secure them to a high ledge for an optimal cure, but that's considered cruel and can have legal repercussions even if the patients sign a waiver."

"Shit," said Twitchell, feeling dizzy as the cars moved beneath him. "Don't they—these acro-people—don't they freak out?"

"Initially, yes, there's quite a bit of panic. Some pass out, a few vomit. But eventually, with this hyper-immersion in their greatest terror, they emerge phobia-free."

"You couldn't do it gradual?"

"Very astute of you. Traditionally, that's how phobias have been treated, with exposures to the feared thing or situation being incrementally increased over time. People with a fear of flying, for example, might start off merely looking at a picture of an airplane or handling a toy plane, then progress to driving to the airport and driving back. The entire process up to the time the patient actually flies can take months, years! With my method, which I call flooding, a cure can be almost immediate."

"And people pay for this?"

"Not yet. Flooding is still in the experimental stages. That's why I rely so heavily on volunteers and on people whose phobias can be easily reproduced. Fear of God, for instance, which is called theophobia, or antlophobia, fear of floods, would be difficult, if not impossible, to replicate."

"But there's no one in here?"

"Not today, no. But there's a patient undergoing treatment across the hall—one of the noisy ones, I'm afraid. Come take a look."

The next room contained several large dividers arranged to create a small enclosure at its center. A plump nurse, looking bored and doodling in the margin of a magazine, sat near the door with a clipboard.

Behind the screens, someone was gasping softly: "Breathe, one, two, three; breathe, one, two, three."

"Try to relax, Eddie, only seventeen more minutes," the nurse called out cheerfully.

Davenport beckoned Twitchell closer. Peering between two of the screens, he was braced to see something upsetting, even repugnant. Instead, he saw a pale young man with a dark mustache and beard seated in a chair. And another pale young man and another...the screens were mirrors and the reflection was reflected back and forth, multiplying the subject into infinity.

"Breathe," moaned the young man and his images. "Breathe."

"I don't get it," said Twitchell, when they were outside in the hall. "Mirrors?"

"Eisoptrophobia," said Davenport. "Fear of mirrors. Very rare, but extremely incapacitating. He can't even go into apublic rest room or try on clothes without a panic attack."

"So you surround the poor dumb fuck with mirrors. Pretty drastic, huh, doc?"

"It works, that's the important point. The human mind can only accept a certain amount of fear. When that's exceeded, it simply whites out, goes numb. When that man's two hours are up, he'll be beyond fear. Mirrors will have lost their power over him."

Twitchell nodded, wondering if the guy would still be able to tie his shoelaces or use a toothbrush.

The next room was in total darkness. Twitchell heard choppy breathing, and a woman's voice repeating the Mirror Man's mantra, "Breathe, one, two, three…" When the door opened, there was a small gasp. Then: "Dr. Davenport, is that you? I think I've had enough now. I'm feeling better really, I'm breathing just fine, let's stop this, Dr. Davenport. Dr. Davenport? Pleeeease."

Followed by frantic sobs and curses when Davenport closed the door.

"Don't tell me, doc. Fear of darkness."

"Exactly. Achluophobia. More common than you'd think, especially among women. They're afraid to leave their house at night, sleep with all the lights on. They think they're afraid of crime, but really it's the darkness. That woman hasn't been outside her home at night for seven years.

"One more," said Davenport, "an aichmophobic. Then we'll get down to the business of your own phobia, Mr. Twitchell, whatever it may be."

The aichmophobic turned out to be a woman terrified of sharp objects. She sat at a table covered with knives of various sizes and a small pile of razor blades. Davenport said her fear of sharp objects was associated with the subconscious wish to harm herself. A nurse sitting across from her spoke in a soft, soothing voice, while lightly handling the implements. Every few seconds she carefully touched the blade of a knife against the woman's bare arm, and the woman would flinch as though stung.

"We're doing just fine here," the nurse said as Davenport entered. "We've stopped all that silly screaming, haven't we?"

The woman, who was middle-aged with dyed, flaxen hair, smiled timidly and shuddered as the nurse stroked a razor blade across her wrist.

"Jesus, be careful, you'll cut her!" exploded Twitchell.

He lurched against the table, jostling implements to the floor. The woman's eyes opened wide. She started to sob.

Sick to his stomach, a hand clapped to his mouth, Twitchell stumbled out into the hall. Davenport followed.

"Are you all right?"

"I don't like sharp stuff."

"That's your phobia?"

"No, doc, it's—"

Davenport seemed delighted. "It's nothing to be ashamed of. There's nothing unmasculine about phobic fear. Why, I once treated a football player who was terrified of cats. His girlfriend had three cats which she refused to part with and—"

"You stuck him in a cage with a lion?"

"Not quite. But put it this way, he's cured. As you will be, too, when I'm finished."

A faint, not-very-pleasant smile played on Davenport's lips. It was a refined, more sophisticated version of the smile Twitchell knew all too well, the bully's smile, smug and arrogant and condescending.

"You get off on scarin' people, don't you, doc? You're kinda like them old-time torture guys, them Inquisitioners."

"Nothing of the kind. I only—"

"The rush this must give you. Scaring people to death with a shit-load of whatever they fear the most. Some power trip, huh, doc?"

Davenport only widened that know-it-all smirk, like he thought Twitchell was paying him a compliment. "You attack me because you're afraid, Mr. Twitchell. Something in that last room upset you badly. I think that's where we need to resume our interview."

They returned to Davenport's office where Twitchell slouched in the chair, his head in his hands. His stomach felt like it was perched on a seasaw. He could still see the blade of the knife as it lightly indented the blonde's tissue white skin.

"Lemme get this straight, doc. If I tell you what my phobia is you're gonna find some way to, like, super overexpose me to what scares me, so I'll either get used to it or go fucking crazy."

"The former, I assure you. You're basically not an unstable man. I don't do phobic flooding with seriously disturbed individuals."

"But I killed somebody, doc."

"I know your case, Mr. Twitchell. Your foreman belittled you. A grudge had built up. I'm not condoning murder, but in this case, I'd say you're simply a very volatile man. And I imagine you'd not only like the extra privileges you've been promised, but to be relieved of your phobia as well."

Twitchell leaned back, took in a deep breath. Maybe the doctor had something here. He was scared, sure, scared shitless, but wasn't it worth it to take the chance? To not go through life like a quaking, craven sissy. To not live in terror of being humiliated by people finding out about his problem.

"My phobia, doc,—it's kind of womanish. McGee gave me a lot of grief about it."

"And so you killed him."

"Well, ya gotta understand, McGee was makin' fun of me all the time. Cause of my size, I'm just 5'4", and my hands—McGee used to call 'em girly hands—small feet, shit, my dick's not exactly stud-sized, but it gets the job done.

"But the worst was one day I was eating lunch across from McGee and—well, he had this can of peaches in his lunch box and, openin' it up, he—fuck, this ain't easy, doc."

He looked down at his trembling, effeminate little hands. How Davenport must be laughing at him now, the way McGee had laughed.

"Take your time, Mr. Twitchell. No need to be afraid."

"I ain't afraid."

"Your hands—"

"I *told* you the shaking's a hereditary thing."

"Of course."

"Well, McGee cut his hand on the can top and he's bleedin' all over the goddamn Cling peaches. And my head just spins and next thing I know I puked up my lunch and then passed out cold."

Davenport nodded grandly, reached for his pen.

"So that's it! Hematophobia. Not uncommon. Nothing to be ashamed of, I assure—"

The razor blade that Twitchell had palmed off the table in the aichmophobic's room sliced a grin in the thick meat under Davenport's jaw. Thick crimson jetted out of Davenport's jugular, spattering the desk and wall like a Jackson Pollack painted in gore.

"Breathe," muttered Twitchell, as he'd heard the others do. "Breathe, it'll pass, breathe, one, two, three."

Gouts of blood splashed Twitchell's hands as Davenport sagged against him. His stomach lurched and bars of darkness shimmied across his vision.

"Breathe, one, two, three."

The room swayed around Twitchell, then gradually righted itself. Davenport lay face up, his throat pumping. Twitchell poked a finger into the gory pool. Smeared some across his tongue. Salt and copper, not entirely unpleasant. Some of the queasiness returned, but he breathed his way through it.

In the hallway, Twitchell heard a heavy tread that could only have been Olsun's and realized the guard must have finally checked the monitor. He stepped behind the door, the razor ready.

A smile split his face—little Twitchy-Pie the Giant Killer was going for number three.

But he couldn't resist shouting as Olsun stormed through the door and he opened his second scarlet gusher of the day, "Hey, Olsun, I'm cured!"

SLIPS

"My name's Rita, and I'm a sex addict," said the chubby brunette with the pierced nostril and the Guns 'N Roses t-shirt.

In a chair at the back of the Lafayette Street Unitarian Church basement, Darren chorused "Hi Rita" along with the twenty or so others at the meeting of Sex Addicts Anonymous. He sipped his coffee and kept some pamphlets on sex addiction ready to hold across his broad lap in case his dick got a notion to sit up and sniff for pussy while the woman told her tale.

"Sex was always my drug of choice," Rita was saying. "I could never say no, even when I was being treated like shit, even when I knew I was risking my life and my health having sex with a different guy every night…"

As far as Darren was concerned, these SAA meetings were the equivalent of a sexual smorgasbord. Wilder than porn. Hotter than whores. That stuff was fake, desire bought or simulated. SAA was real, the people and their incredible stories of addiction to s/m, b/d, group sex, animal sex, sex with tuberous vegetables and albino dwarves, every kind of erotic kick you could imagine.

Hell, he'd *pay* to attend these meetings, and they were open to anybody willing to come in and admit to being a sex addict.

Darren would have declared himself a transvestite Republican nun if it were necessary for admission to SAA.

"…there's not very much I didn't do when I was acting out my addiction," Rita went on. She spoke with a flat, Midwestern twang. Although she was probably still in her twenties, her deadpan expression, troubled eyes the color of weak coffee, and the short but noticeable scar at the left corner of her mouth gave her the frayed-at-the-edges appearance of rummage sale goods.

"…I worked the streets for awhile, then I got involved in making porn movies. The kinkier the better, as far as I was concerned…"

That sent Darren's imagination into overdrive. He shifted in the narrow folding chair, trying to rearrange his bulk to a more com-

101

fortable position. With over two hundred pounds packed onto his 5'8" frame and a bald shiny pate like a speckled atoll adrift in a shallow sea of brown fringe, he looked more like a gone-to-seed bouncer than manager of the appliance department at the Cherry Creek Sears.

And he certainly didn't look like anyone who would be called the Inquisitioner, although that was how he'd begun to fancy thinking of himself lately.

"...My ambition was to experience every sexual act possible.

But even in porn, there are a few things you can't do, and my goal was to do *everything*..."

The first half of the meeting was devoted to a speaker, who told his or her story, the second half to some group discussion of a topic such as self-esteem or how to avoid a slip, that is, a backslide into self-destructive sexual behavior. Darren never shared information about himself. On those rare occasions when he was called on to speak, he gave a fake name and said, "Tonight I just want to listen." No one objected. No one pried. They probably figured he would "open up" and talk when he felt ready.

Like to make you open up for me, you nasty bitch.

"I suppose I'm lucky I wasn't killed by some nutcase..."

Sometimes Darren saw himself as a kind of priest, listening quietly, patiently, hard-on in hand, while the woman, (men were not contenders—sorry, all you faggot bondage freaks) told her story, meek and penitent as a child saying bedtime prayers.

Don't worry, I won't hurt you. I won't even touch you. See, I'm just going to touch myself. I only want to listen.

"I've been in SAA a year now, and I'm trying to make a life for myself that doesn't include degrading and dangerous sex. I'm going to beauty school, learning how to do make-up, hair..."

He was prudent. He never hit the same meeting more than three times if he didn't find a woman that he wanted. After a "date," he'd drop out for a month or two, then resume going to SAA meetings in another part of Denver. Eventually, Darren figured he might have to move to another city, but that was no problem, since SAA was a country-wide organization, based on the principles of Alcoholics Anonymous. It amused Darren to think that, whereas at one time, he might have had to spend days tracking down some after-hours sex club, bribing cabbies to take him to some seedy part of town where both his life and self-respect would be in jeopardy, now the self-help movement made it possible to find a group of self-pro-claimed sex junkies in any city from Wabash to Des Moines.

Nor were these people shy about telling, in dick-stiffening detail, the degradations that had brought them, humbled and con-trite, to SAA. Darren had virtually memorized the words of the blonde cellist he'd "dated" not long ago. She claimed to have mas-saged herself to orgasm against her instrument in full view of two hundred concert-goers ("...and then I rubbed myself against the edge of the instrument and—no, please don't do that again, please no—") and the middle-aged, overweight artist so addicted to auto-erotic asphyxiation that she almost killed herself when a jerry-rigged noose failed to release after she lost consciousness ("I used some pantyhose and tied them to a light fixture, and—but I'm *telling* you the truth. Don't hurt me anymore! Don't *do* that!")

Darren forced his attention back to Rita. Sometimes when he started remembering the ones he had on tape, it was hard to con-centrate on the one at hand.

"I think of every fantasy I ever had, there was only one I never acted out. And that was one reason I came to SAA. I was on a search for something more forbidden, fantasizing about doing something that even I found disgusting. I knew I had to get help."

Confess to me, thought Darren, *and I'll give you all the help you'll ever need.*

When the meeting ended, he left quickly, before the woman he had chosen to be his next "date" had a chance to see his face.

《《——》》

He'd been sitting in his Cutlass for fifteen minutes, beginning to fret that there might be more than one exit from the church base-ment, when Rita emerged alone, getting into a late-model Camry and driving east on Ralston Road. He waited while she shopped briefly in a Wynn-Dixie along the way, then followed her to a low income townhouse in a subdivision of Arvada. It was dark by now, hard pellets of drizzle beginning to strike the windshield. Hugging her grocery bags to her chest, she ran to the porch, unlocked her door and was gone.

Darren jotted down the address, went home, and crawled into bed with his Walkman and one of his tapes. Sheila, the check-out girl who liked black dudes and who'd died rather suddenly—he thought her heart had given out—was tonight's featured attraction.

"...how many black dudes have you fucked?"

A soft, shuddering breath. Then, barely audible, "Fifty, sixty, I'm not sure."

"You'll have to speak up."

"Sixty."

Screaming. "Liar, fucking cunt liar!"

"A hundred, two hundred!"

"Liar!"

"No, please, pl——-"

Then the soft, wet muffled sounds that Darren's body was so attuned to that he could ejaculate almost on cue, the thunderous release of his own passion set to the throaty, sucky sounds of suffocation.

«《——》»

On Sunday morning, when he went to Mass as usual, Darren thanked God for making him steadfast against the indecencies of fornication. The fact that he didn't touch the women he tape-recorded and killed proved he wasn't a sex addict himself. Not only did he abstain from fucking his "dates", he seldom made physical contact except to heave his bulk upon them, hold them down while he used the pillow to help him extract the truth.

No, he didn't need the coarse, cheap stimulation of the flesh to satisfy himself, like other people did. He was different. Better. He sought only the truth. A natural born Inquisitioner.

On his way out of church, he stepped into a confessional. His sins were mingy ones, probably disappointing to the priest.

Some covetousness, a bit of gluttony at Denny's Two-for-One Special the other night, and lust, yes, he confessed to masturbating, wondering if the priest was secretly aroused.

When he was done, he felt cleansed, uplifted, made spiritually sound.

Ready now. In mind and soul and body.

Ready to hear Rita's confession.

《《—》》

Her studio apartment, identified as the residence of R.E. LoBiando on the mailbox, was potentially accessible through either of two ground-floor windows, one visible from the street, the other blocked by an overgrown hedge. By now Darren had observed her comings and goings for several days and knew when to expect her home.

Wearing a Sears shirt and cap purloined from the supply room, he was ready to pretend to be taking window measurements for the installment of an air conditioner should anybody question what he was doing.

No one did, nor did the window offer more than token resistance to his prybar. Hefting his bulk through it was the difficult part. Once that was accomplished, he had only to wait for her.

The tiny apartment, he noted sourly, was a pigsty. Clothes scattered on the floor, food-encrusted dishes heaped in the sink, ashtrays overflowing like miniature Mt. Vesuvius's. The single table obviously served as her desk. He remembered now she said she was in beauty school: issues of *Today's Make-up* and *Modern Hair* lay in a colorful spill across the table.

Her bed occupied an alcove off the main room. It was queen-sized, unmade, and obviously doubled as her eating area. A grease-slick pizza box with two slices left sat on the floor by the bed. Chinese take-out cartons, noodles trailing entrailishly down the sides, were stacked on a bedside table. Grubby tableware and a plastic drink tumbler on the floor.

So Rita was not just a slut, but a slob, too, Darren noted as he slipped the tape recorder out of his pocket and placed it by the bed. Then in the hallway, footsteps. Another second, just long enough for him to step behind the bathroom door, and she was inside.

He heard her pause to slide the chain to, relished the irony of that.

He even let her use the toilet, listening to the musical pinging of her urine in the bowl, the flush that followed, before he came from behind the door as she was pulling down her skirt and said quite reasonably, "Don't make a sound and I won't hurt you."

Without missing a beat, she pivoted and grabbed for an aerosol can of hairspray on the sink, aiming for his eyes, but he ducked and backhanded her hard, knocking her to the floor. She lay glaring at him with more fury than fear, the scar at the side of her mouth a thin, twitchy line.

"You brought that on yourself," he said. "Now I'll tell you again. I don't want to hurt you. Just talk to you."

"Get the hell out of here."

He put his foot down on her hand, enough pressure to get the point across. He hoped she realized how easy it would be to pulverize the delicate bones in her fingers and wrist.

"You don't understand. I ask the questions. You answer. Simple, isn't it. All right?"

"What quest—" His heel ground flesh and tendon. "—I mean, yes, whatever you say."

"That's better." He took his weight off her hand. "Now go lie on the bed. You don't have to remove your clothing, by the way. I don't intend to rape you."

She got up, eyes flashing toward the front door, the chain. He could see her weighing the odds. He hadn't shown her any weapon, had only used force when she fought back. But he was big man; he could crush her with his weight alone. He guessed she'd figured that out by now.

"Clear off the bed," he said evenly. "The sheets, too. I don't intend to sit on filthy bedding."

"It isn't—"

He raised his hand. She flinched, went silent.

"Very good. You're learning."

Slowly, methodically as a bag lady doing the Thorazine shuffle, she removed reading and eating matter from the bed, littering the floor with the discards of her various meals. A pair of chopsticks clattered from the Chinese take-out carton, dragging limp snowpeas to the woven rug.

"Now," he said, "when she was sitting on the bed, "tell me about the things you talked about at the SAA meeting last week."

In quick succession, surprise, outrage, and terror strobed across her face, were replaced by the protective blank mask. "But this time, I want to know *everything*. And no lies. Lie and you won't like what happens."

"I don't know what—"

With the flat of his meaty hand, he shoved her back, grabbed the pillow next to her head, pressed it over her face.

She arched and flopped and sputtered. He put his weight on her. Counted—not too quickly—to ten.

When he removed the pillow, she was ashen, gasping, little bubbles of saliva foaming from between her lips.

The recorder got it all. He bent toward her. "I won't hurt you as long as you don't lie. Now, shall we begin?"

He decided to begin the interview by asking about her lesbian encounters. How many dykes had she fucked? Did she use a dildo? What color and size? Did she go down on them? What was the taste like? The smell?

"I don't know. I don't remem—"

"Dammit, Goddamit, I said don't lie!" He put his whole weight on the pillow, counted five and let her breath, not because he was being generous but because he couldn't wait to see the terror in her eyes. The caught, desperate terror of a person who'd do anything, anything at all, whose powerlessness was shamefully, nakedly exposed.

"All right, but let me breath. I can't think if I can't breathe. I've been with fifteen, twenty women. At least."

He leaned close enough to smell the lunch meat on her breath. "Are you sure? You don't want to lie to me, do you?"

"No."

He raised the pillow, held it six inches above her face while he straddled her chest. "You don't want to make me mad."

"I used dildos on most of them."

Two inches from her face.

"Big dildos, rubber ones with bumps and ridges along the shaft."

She cringed into the mattress. The pillow fell to the side.

"Good. I believe you." He reached down, unzipped his jeans beneath the swoop of belly. White hairy flesh, like yeasted dough, popped into view, then his cock, which was a tiny replica of its owner, short and stocky, pink as a baby's butt at the crown. He grabbed it joy-stick-style with one hand, held the pillow with the other. "Keep talking. Make it interesting enough, and you can breathe."

He got forty minutes worth of tape. She stayed conscious, and sometimes he'd catch her eyes wandering—to the door, the phone, he could almost hear her mind clicking wildly for an escape opening—but her eyes were going glassy and the quality of her voice was degenerating badly, getting sore and throaty-sounding from the gasping. He could tell she lied to him, too, exaggerating some things, downplaying others, so he had no choice but to keep up the punishment.

Not enough to kill her, though. Not before he heard her full confession.

"Now tell me what you left out at the SAA meeting. What fantasy was it you didn't get to do? Wait, I'll bet I know. You wanted to fuck a dog."

She looked at him, cringing with sick dread when he raised the pillow.

"No."

"Liar."

"No, I—yes, yes, I wanted to do a dog, a big Doberman. That was it."

"And lick his dick? You wanted to lick the dog's dick?"

"Yes, yes,"

"What else? A child, wasn't it? You wanted to have sex with a little boy."

"No."

He mashed the pillow down hard onto her face. "You're lying. Deep down everybody wants to do a kid. Everybody wants to fuck anything that'll hold still. People are no damned good."

She thrashed beneath him, twisting, kicking. He held the pillow to the count of ten. Released her. The tape recorder by the bed picked up her desperate struggling to breath.

"You going to tell the truth?"

He put the pillow back before she had a chance to answer.

Began the count again. One and…

When he removed the pillow this time, she lay limp, rasping like a gaffed fish. Her head and arms were slung back off the edge of the bed, tarty little dress rucked up around her thighs so the white lace of her underpants was visible, stubble of hair on her calves, faint odor of fear and sour sweat wafting off her. Disgusted by her immodesty, he yanked the dress down.

"Come on, wake up. We're not through yet."

Oh, shit, sometimes he got carried away. He couldn't let her die yet. Not until he'd extracted the full confession.

Her limp body looked in danger of sliding off the bed. He reached down and took a handful of dress, pulled up—

—saw only the gleaming teak shaft of the chopstick she'd grabbed up off the floor—a monosodium-glutamate-poisoned punji stick—before it skewered his left eye. And was twisted, scraping socket, scooping out optic nerve like the last tasty morsels in the bottom of the carton of moo goo gai pan.

He screamed, flailed out for her throat, equilibrium now sacrificed to agony, fell off the bed. The chopstick popped out of his eye, bringing with it a pea-sized gobbet of iris. He clamped his fists to his face, a strand of pink tears bubbling from the lacerated eye.

Giving her time to raid the empty pizza box and slam a cheese-encrusted knife upward into the soft flesh of his throat while she rode him to the rug like a dying bull.

"You want to know what my fucking fantasy is?" she shouted as blood and dried mozzarella dripped onto the floor. "You want to know?"

But he died before she could tell him.

《《—》》

In SAA it would be considered a slip, a lapse back into unwanted behavior. Rita LoBiando no longer gave a shit. Besides, if she got honest, she'd admit she'd been working up to a slip ever since she enrolled in beauty school. She just didn't expect the opportunity to satisfy her obsession to come along so soon.

She tugged down the corpse's pants and smiled. Rolled a Trojan over his boner.

Dead men weren't going to be half bad, she decided. They never hit you and sometimes they even had hard-ons.

At the Chapel of Roses Mortuary, where she was supposed to start work as a hairdresser and cosmetologist in two weeks, dead men were the only kind.

THE ENGLISH TEACHER

I was sitting on the front steps crying, while the movers carried out the last of the furniture, when I saw my old high school English teacher, Mr. Mathias, striding across the front lawn. For a second, I couldn't believe it. Martinsville, Virginia, is a good hour's drive from Blacksburg, where I grew up and went to high school. Except for the odd nightmare now and then, I hadn't thought about Earl Mathias for years.

I figured he was dead.

He deserved to be.

But here he came, brazen as day, grinning his absurdly jovial grin, his grey hair long and ratty-looking, at once unkempt and avuncular, kind of a Captain Kangaroo Does Skid Row Show.

"Cheryl, Cheryl Booth," he beamed, extending a hand so large and soft and shapeless it resembled a flesh-colored oven mitt. "I saw you from my car. Thought I recognized you."

The brass of the man was unnerving—how dare he! I tried to smile and hoped he wouldn't realize I'd been crying.

My boys, Adam and Mark, came tearing around the corner of the house in pursuit of a Frisbee.

"Yours sons?"

I nodded, ignoring the opportunity to make introductions. Names are powerful. I had no wish for Earl Mathias to know my children's' names.

"Married, are you?"

"Was."

"Oh," he nodded. "I understand."

You understand nothing.

My hands began to tingle, adrenalin spreading its intimate fire throughout my body, tempting me to leap up and claw that leer from Earl Mathias' eyes.

"Ma'am, we need you to sign this."

I looked up and saw the movers were finished loading the van.

The boys' bikes were being lifted in, and I could see the head posts of the brass bed that I'd thought Mac would surely ask for. He hadn't, though. His girlfriend couldn't fuck him properly, I guess, on the bed his wife had slept in.

For a second, crimson stars spun behind my eyes. "Excuse me," I said to Earl Mathias.

"Wait." He reached out and draped a hot, heavy arm around my shoulder. His breath reeked of some over-sweet breakfast confection, maple syrup and cinnamon. "Remember that paper you never finished? I'd still like to see it, Cheryl. I'm not going to forget."

The crimson seemed to brighten briefly before it spiraled into black. The next thing I knew, the movers were standing over me, one of them asking in a worried voice, "Lady, do you want me to call a doctor?"

Earl Mathias had gone.

《《—》》

"Why didn't you like that fat guy?" asked Mark a few days later when we were still trying to get settled in the apartment I'd rented across town.

"What man?"

"The porker who was standing there right before you went—" He stiffened and did a felled tree imitation onto the carpet—*"ker-PLOP."*

"What makes you think I didn't like him?"

"You looked at him the way you used to look at Dad. After he divorced us."

《《—》》

But Mark was wrong. I had come to hate my ex-husband, but I never feared him. Earl Mathias, I feared.

The term paper he referred to had been the final one of my senior year. Nothing particularly unusual about it except that, unlike my other assignments, which I completed in the mediocre fashion of a "B" student more interested in boys than in Tennyson or Hardy, this one I never turned in.

112

I still remembered writing two or three paragraphs and getting stuck. Terminal writer's block. Like butting my naked brain against cement. I wasn't lazy and I didn't lack for time

—I simply couldn't bring myself to write the paper.

The day before the paper was due, I stopped by Mr. Mathias' office, a dinky cubicle on the third floor next to the library. Mathias folded his boneless-looking hands on his belly and smiled at me like a dowdy Santa Claus out of costume and down on his luck.

I asked if I could do a different paper. Mathias shook his head with mock gloom.

"When I was giving out assignments, Cheryl, I chose this one because it seemed right for you."

That seemed the grimmest of sentences. My knees and chin began to tremble. I tried to wipe my eyes, and my glasses fell off. One lens cracked against the edge of Mr. Mathias' desk. I burst into heartfelt sobs.

"There now," said Mr. Mathias. He stood up and closed the door. His left hand scooped a handful of bonbons from the candy dish on his desk, while his right slid briefly inside his jacket. When he sat down again, I was stunned to see that he'd released his penis and that it stood straight up and wiggled like a chastising finger telling me I'd been a naughty girl. His meat was grub-pale with a tiny glistening bubble of wetness, like spittle, at the crown.

"If you want an easier assignment, dear, I suppose I might consider it. You'll have to earn it, though."

He reached up and clasped the back of my neck, drew me down toward that glistening stob. I was paralyzed with terror and revulsion so profound that I almost vomited as my lips neared his slick, pallid flesh.

"No, please, don't do this."

"Just make me feel good," he said through a mouthful of chocolate, "and I'll give you another assignment. Something you'll find more agreeable, perhaps, more palatable."

I shook free of Mr. Mathias' hand and stared up into his small, murky eyes, and I realized something that compounded the horror I already felt: Mr. Mathias, whomever that person had been, wasn't in there anymore. Mr. Mathias was long gone, eaten away like an

113

apple cored out by worms and something else entirely, something ravenous and foul now blinked from inside Mr. Mathias' cockroach-brown eyes.

"No!"

He gripped my head with both hands then, forced my face into his groin. My lips, pinched tight together, brushed the damp, silken head of his erection.

"Open," he hissed. "Open your—"

I opened my mouth to accommodate him. Mr. Mathias howled as my teeth seized the mushroom-like dome of white flesh. Masticated chocolate spewed from his mouth, and his cock fainted away, small and limp like a rotted tubor.

I threw open the door and ran up the hall and kept running, out of the building and home.

«« — »»

I never went back to Mr. Mathias' class after that, but at the end of the year he still gave me a "B". I figured it was because I never told anyone what he'd done. How could I, though? I told myself it was because I knew nobody'd believe me, but the truth was I was afraid of what Mr. Mathias might do.

Only once I ran into him. It was at graduation. I was standing with some other kids, Mom and Dad snapping pictures, when he suddenly walked up and put his arm around me, beaming into my Dad's camera.

As I winced beneath the power of his grip, he whispered, so close to my ear that no one else could hear, "The paper, Cheryl, I've not forgotten it. Sooner or later, you'll have to turn it in."

And he kissed me, a small, sweet-smelling peck upon the cheek that was like an evil promise.

All that summer I lived in fear that somehow Earl Mathias would come and get me, that I'd awaken with his weight upon me, his obscene meat penetrating my face.

But then I went off to college in Kentucky, married Mac and came back to live in Virginia. Mac made good money as an accountant with R. J. Reynolds Tobacco Company. We had a lovely house, expensive trips, a perfect marriage. Or so I thought. My husband appeared to be devoted, my two sons were a joy.

I thought I had no cause to worry about Mr. Mathias ever again. Until that day when he came back into my life.

《《—》》

Before long, though, I was too preoccupied with other matters to give much thought to the unpleasant encounter with Earl Mathias. I hated being alone, despised the small apartment where the boys and I now lived, and spent much of my free time fantasizing about ways to punish Mac for destroying my safe and comfortable life.

Against my wishes, the Court had appointed Mac visiting rights to the boys. In my opinion, a man who leaves his family for another woman should never be allowed to see his children again. The judge thought differently. Fine, then, Mac could visit them all he wanted. We'd see how often he found time, however, when the boys and I moved three thousand miles away.

The trip to California was expensive and exhausting. I ended up selling or giving away most of the furniture. There were a few pieces I knew Mac treasured and these I graciously returned to him, after giving them a generous shellacking of acid.

In early April, we drove to L.A., where I got a job as a receptionist at a bank. It didn't pay enough, and Mac communicated through his lawyer that, since I'd violated the terms of the divorce by moving out of state, he would continue to send child support, but no alimony.

The boys were no help at all. They badgered me to let them visit their Dad. They behaved as though nothing had happened, like Mac hadn't left us to run off with some little slut with an MBA and a cash register between her thighs. Then in May, Mac called to say he was getting married. Would I allow the boys to fly back to Virginia for the wedding?

That was the night I broke Adam's arm. It was an accident, of course. Adam is my son, my darling baby.

But he has Mac's quick, furtive eyes and when he screamed at me that he wanted to see Daddy, I grabbed him and slung him against the wall. He twisted in some awkward fashion—I still don't understand—and I heard the bone crack and saw his face go ashen.

I told the doctor in the Emergency Room that he fell off a swing. Adam just sat there looking scared. He didn't contradict me.

That night, I went to a bar, intending to have just one drink, and drank so much so quickly that soon I had to put my head down on my arms. I heard someone slide onto the stool next to me. He smelled of cloves and Hershey Bars, more like a bakery than a bar. I thought of children lured into cars with candy bars and never seen again, of Halloween chocolate spiked with rat poison, and even before I lifted my head, I knew it was Earl Mathias.

He smiled as if I were some long lost daughter.

"You look exhausted, dear."

"I'm fine."

"I didn't know you drank."

The bartender came over. Earl Mathias ordered club soda.

"Life's so unjust, isn't it," he said. "Call it karma, call it Fate, sometimes it just doesn't seem to play fair. Your marriage, for example, what a pity."

I wasn't the little girl he'd intimidated years ago, and I was too drunk to be afraid. "What the fuck are you doing here?

Are you following me? Did you get run out of town for child molesting?"

His eyes got small and mean and piggish, and I glimpsed it for the second time—that Other, that black void that inhabited the skin of Earl Mathias.

"I'm still waiting for that paper," he said. "Sooner or later, you're going to have to hand it in."

I rushed out of the bar. That day I gave up drinking and I swore I'd never lay a hand on Mark or Adam again.

And I didn't. I was the perfect mother.

Until the day that Mac filed for custody of the boys. He said he'd gotten a phone call from a man claiming to be an old family friend. Said I'd broken Adam's arm, that I was an abusive, unfit mother.

Unfit!

The fucking bastard. I loved my sons. Was it my fault I loathed the man whose DNA conjoined with mine to make them? That every day I had to look at them, I saw Mac's eyes, his mouth, that irritating dimple of his that the caprices of genetics had somehow replicated on Adam's chin.

I sat on the back steps of our miserable motel apartment, crying my eyes out. When the shadow fell across my lap, I didn't even have to look to know who it must be.

But this time I was prepared. I'd thought about it. I knew what I had to do.

The boys were at school.

I pulled Mr. Mathias into the apartment and fell to my knees. I fumbled with his zipper. His cock lolled out at me, thick and pale as an albino eel raised in some lightless cavern. The sight no longer repulsed me as it had all those years ago. I wasn't innocent anymore, was no longer saving myself for the right man, who would love me and protect me and be faithful. I no longer cared what I had to do as long as I got Mathias to leave me alone.

I sucked him into my mouth like his dick was made of white Godiva chocolate, made love with my lips and throat and tongue, not to the man, but to that swollen image of him that bobbed up like a nasty little idol from the frizzy hair at his groin. He gave a cry and thrust down my throat. His cum pumped toward my tonsils. I thought of the slime a slug leaves behind it on the leaves, glistening mucus. I turned and threw up on the rug. When I was done retching, I heard Marthias slipping out the door. I scrambled after him.

"Wait! Are we even now?"

He looked down at me with cold pleasure. "You had your chance once long ago, my dear, and you blew it. More to the point, if I recall correctly, your mistake was that you *didn't.*

I'm sorry but it's too late now. I'm a busy man. I'm not giving out new assignments, just collecting on the old ones, and I'll be back tomorrow for yours. But thank you anyway, at least over the years you've learned to suck a cock."

《《——》》

That night I sat up almost til dawn writing the paper. It wasn't necessary to go to the library and find the book again. I still remembered almost every word. The play had made that profound an impression on me, touched a nerve of pure terror deep inside me for reasons I only now began to understand.

The next morning, Mathias came around.

He chuckled. "I always wondered why you had such trouble with this. Euripides really tells such a gripping tale, so full of passion, drama. I always knew this play suited your temperament."

He glanced at the smeared, gin-stained pages.

"I don't know if you can read it," I said.

"It doesn't matter," said Mathias. "It's not the words I'm interested in."

《《—》》

Because it isn't finished, of course. It hasn't even started.

Mac has got to be punished. Has got to suffer more than he'd ever have imagined possible. I realized it, of course, when I was writing the paper, when I was reliving that other woman's suffering and torment. Feeling her bitterness and betrayal. That this was what I had to do, this was the answer I'd wanted all along, but was afraid to look at.

Euripides knew about justice, about rage and vindictiveness. In his play, he captured it perfectly.

Mac's sons are still sleeping. The tranquilizers I put into their milk last night made sure of that.

I go into the kitchen, get what I need.

Now it begins, with the knife clutched in Medea's hand. Medea moves toward the children's bedroom, where Jason's sons lie sleeping.

Somewhere I can almost hear Mathias laughing. In some hellish cosmic grade book, he's giving me an "A".

THE FAMILY UNDERWATER

It was soon after my fifteenth birthday that I came home from school one day to find that our frame house on the corner of Monument Avenue and Malvern Street had filled up with water all the way to the second-floor ceiling. I don't mean it was *under* water—it was *full* of water, like a toy house that you'd put in the bottom of an aquarium for the guppies to swim through and the bottomsuckers to clean. Inside, my mother and my ten-year-old sister Babette floated from room to room like big soft ballerinas doing a *pas de deux* in soggy slow motion.

I stared through the living room window, afraid to open the front door for fear a torrent of water would rush out, depositing a waterlogged Mom and Babette and all our tacky furniture and used clothing from Second Hand Rose in a big sopping heap on the lawn.

So I hung around outside until Dad staggered home, listing side to side like a ship with an unbalanced cargo, sweat stains the size of volleyballs under his arms and that mean glint in his eyes that suggested his reception that evening at The Tramp Lounge had not been worthy of his stature in Tampa's dominant social class, the Fraternal Order of Drunkards, Bullies, and Buttholes.

But I digress, as Ms. Flannahan in English 202 used to say.

In his own sodden state, Dad didn't even notice the condition of the interior of our house, but opened the door and plunged right into a stationary wall of water, while I gaped through the window. The water didn't seem to distract Dad at all from his mission, which, as usual, was to dump shit onto his nearest and dearest. In that respect, we all functioned at one time or another as toilets.

Tonight, Dad's face was red as a clown's carnation, and his mouth hung open like a piranha with a bad overbite. He was flailing his arms about, but it was all taking place in slow motion, and—best of all—there was almost no sound. Oh, I could hear little gurgles that might have been "goddamn bitch" and "lousy fag bar-

119

tender" but mostly it was just soft, sucky sounds, like a baby's farts, not scary, but almost comical.

Mom scowled and said something that came out of her mouth in a long string of silvery bubbles. It looked like she was puking up pearls or the egg cases of some exotic sea creature.

Then I saw Dad raise his hand and strike Mom alongside the head, but underwater like that, it took about ten seconds for his hand to connect with her jaw, and a good fifteen more for Mom to go down—in slow, graceful silence, her dress floating up high in the water so I could see her blue underpants billowing, her shoulder striking the edge of the coffee table with a muffled, wet *thrump*.

Something tiny and gold, about the size of a corn kernel floated past the window. It took me a minute to realize it was one of Mom's teeth. I took a deep breath, planning to hold it just long enough to drag Mom and Babette out of the house, and I plunged into the submerged living room.

As soon as I entered the water, Dad came at me, his rubbery lips twisted like a riled moray eel, his mouth working but no sound coming out except the glug-glug of bubbles that sounded like the toilet tank when it backs up. He grabbed for me, but before he could hit me, Babette floated by, breast stroking like crazy, her red hair fanning out around her head like a halo of flame. She made a shooshing gesture with one finger, then clasped my hand in a motion so graceful and serene, you'd never have guessed the desperation behind it, and floated up the stairs ahead of me like a drowned angel.

It wasn't until we swam into our room and hid in the closet, hovering up level with the coat hangers that I realized I'd been breathing all along. The water was thick and cold and cloying, like breathing snot, and it took some getting used to, but after a while I didn't notice anymore. I was just grateful for the bizarre fact that I was able to breathe at all.

Those first few weeks adjusting to life underwater were difficult. I slept a lot and had strange, murky dreams in which I drowned and revived and drowned again, but I also began to feel a new and welcome calm, a safe-feeling numbness as if a dentist doing a root canal had missed my gum and shot the Novocain directly into my brain. Cotton candy La-La Land, safe and soft and cushiony, where even the most violent fights erupted in silence and serenity, and blood spilling from my lip or Mom's nose unfurled like gorgeous underwater snakes that slowly dissipated into the pale layers of cornflower blue water. Dad's yelling didn't frighten me, and physical pain, what I felt of it at all, seemed to take place in someone else's body, the sensations distant, like the echo of a train disappearing far down a long tunnel.

I began to regret all those years I'd spent living in the air.

At night, Babette and I would lie together in our submerged bed and whisper back and forth, her bubbles breaking on my nose and mouth like kisses.

"How do you suppose it happened?" I said. "I mean, this isn't possible. For one thing, our house never even kept out a good hard rain—how can it hold in all this water without any of it leaking out?"

"What are you talking about?" said Babette. "Our house has always been full of water. Ever since I was three-years-old. Don't you remember? It filled up with water the day of GrandMa's funeral. Dad got drunk and fell against the coffin, and Mom started screaming at him, and Dad smacked her in the face. When we got home, the house was full of water. I wondered why you never said anything about it."

"Is that why I've never seen you cry? You've been underwater all these years?"

Babette nodded. "I'm sorry. I should have told you. I really thought you were just pretending not to know."

"But that still doesn't explain how it happened—how a house can just fill up with water all by itself."

"Because we need it to be full of water," Babette said.

"So we can live here without going crazy."

If there was a down side to living in a house full of water, it was that, after a while I got used to it. To the silence, the slowness, to swimming or floating from room to room instead of walking. Then, *bam*, it was time to go to school or to church or to the grocery store, and the outside world, full of noise and hard edges and sharp, prickly people would hit me like a brick in the teeth, and all I wanted was to dive back underwater.

What was weird, too, was when someone from outside came over to our house, and there I was, safe under the water, but the visitor wasn't, so we'd be moving in two different worlds, a creature of the land and a creature of the sea, hopelessly miscommunicating. After a while I realized that, except for Mom and Babette, it was easier just to be alone.

I remember one disaster that happened right around my first underwater Thanksgiving. I let this boy I liked, Luke Marshak, come over to watch a video. I knew it was a mistake, but Mom had been nagging me to have my friends over, so I did it to appease her. So right in the middle of *The Matrix Revisited,* Dad burst in, floated into the antique hatrack and knocked it flat, then did a kind of underwater imitation of an airplane with only one engine trying to take off. He was swinging his arms around, careening into lamps and picture frames. Objects were sinking slowly toward the floor, a glass lamp shattering in silence, stained-glass shards floating up toward the ceiling, gorgeous as a splintered rainbow, and a tiny fleck of rainbow nicked Luke right above the eye. Big shiny drops of crimson floated out of his forehead and stained the water as Dad went down with a big muffled *flump* onto the floor.

I was so used to this by now, I hardly noticed, but Luke turned the color of skim milk and ran outside like a skinny monkey hopped up on meth. All I could think was what a nerd he was to jump around like that when all he had to do was lie back and float.

I thought I had adapted pretty well to my underwater world until the day Dad ate Babette. Mom was upstairs floating around in the attic, doing the spring cleaning. Dad was downstairs watching professional wrestling on TV, well on his way to replacing all the blood in his body with beer. I was making like Mike Nelson on the old *Sea Hunt* reruns, finning languidly as a porpoise, doing slow-motion somersaults in my room.

Suddenly Babette gave a screech that was sharp and terrifying even underwater. I swam downstairs in time to see Dad on the floor with Babette pinned underneath him. The water around the bottom of her shorts was turning red. She squirmed away, but Dad caught onto her ankles.

Babette began to swim, swimming and screaming, when suddenly Dad's body stiffened and darkened and elongated. Fins sprouted from his spine and belly, and he became a shark, a great white shark with hideous metallic-colored jaws and eyes that looked like they'd been plucked from a deep-frozen corpse. He opened his mouth and sucked Babette in. He gulped her feet and legs down his throat, then her waist, then her just-budding breasts. The water in the living room churned scarlet. Morsels of what looked like albacore tuna, but that had to be flesh, floated past my face. I couldn't think, couldn't fight, couldn't swim, and Babette's skull was being crushed like an empty beer can—I saw her eyes, glassy and huge, full of terror as her face slid down into his maw, and then our Father the Great White Shark looked toward me and focused on me his unspeakable hunger, that gluttonous urge to devour and destroy.

Without hesitating a moment, I opened a window, took a deep breath, swam outside into the air and—fell into the zinnia border and the bright, loud outside world of sharp edges and noise, where I couldn't swim anymore, so I got to my feet and I ran, I ran for my life.

«« — »»

A funny thing about how you change when you've lived under—water. The world of light and air never feels right, never quite works. It's like being E.T. for the rest of your life, always searching for a home you can't quite remember and aren't sure you even liked, but the only place that ever felt "normal."

I spent quite a few years in the air world. I hitchhiked to Phoenix and lived on the street for a while, then moved into a shelter for runaway kids, finished high school, and got a job selling ads for a radio station. With a little effort, I learned not to blow bubbles or try to breaststroke across a room, because people would look at me funny. After a while, you'd never have thought I grew up in any place but the air.

Then one evening, coming home after work, I saw a blond boy with a cigarette and a smirk leaning up against the laundromat on the corner. Hard raptor eyes, a ripe, biteable mouth with just a faint trace of cruelty at the corners, a lump in his Levi's that made my heart melt down all slick and hot and wet into my underpants.

I went home with him.

I wasn't disappointed.

His name was Darius. His apartment was a walk-up on the third floor above a liquor store. The apartment was underwater. He opened the door and swam inside. I swam in behind him. We fucked like fish, in silence and cold-blooded splendor, while the water protected us, kept us separate, a buffer through which hate and fear and violence barely registered. Where blood was beautiful and pain an interesting diversion.

I knew I had come home.

ABOUT THE AUTHOR:

LUCY TAYLOR is the author of seven novels, including *Dancing with Demons, Spree, Nailed, Saving Souls, Eternal Hearts,* and the Stoker-award winning *The Safety of Unknown Cities.* Her stories have appeared in over a hundred magazines and anthologies, including *The Mammoth Book of Historical Erotica, The Best of Cemetery Dance, Twentieth Century Gothic, The Year's Best Fantasy and Horror,* and the *Century's Best Horror Fiction.*

Most recently her work has appeared in *The Mammoth Book of Horror presents The Best of Lucy Taylor, Danse Macabre, Exotic Gothic 5,* and the *Best Horror of the Year #5.*

Taylor lives in Pismo Beach, CA, where she volunteers with cat rescue organization, attends Buddhist retreats, and plots daring escapes to exotic and fantastical places.

ABOUT THE COVER ARTIST:

BILL MUNSTER is a retired high school English teacher. For nearly thirty years he was the editor and publisher of Footsteps magazine, as well as special edition chapbooks by such horror writers like T.E.D. Klein, Ray Bradbury, Clive Barker, Harlan Ellison and many more. In a more mainstream vein Bill wrote a monthly column for four years on writing tips for high school students in the magazine Literary Cavalcade, published by Scholastic. Bill also produced the first study of writer Dean R. Koontz titled *The Dean Koontz Companion.* This edition was eventually replaced by *Discovering Dean Koontz* from Borgo Press. Bill spends most of his time now creating illustrative images in Photoshop. Needless to say, his taste leans towards the dark side. He has written two novels, that will be published under the Borgo banner in the near future. He also has an illustrated book that he published that's due out by the end of March 2013. Bill lives in upstate New York with his wife Marie, and their daughter Kacie. His son Johnathan and his wife Ashley live nearby and are expecting their first child in September 2013.

THE SILENCE BETWEEN THE SCREAMS

BY LUCY TAYLOR

The Silence Between the Screams features cover art by Rick Sardinha.

First Edition Hard Cover ISBN 1892950642 $39.95
Trade Paperback   ISBN 1892950650 $10.95

A Silence Between The Screams is a collection of original short fiction that also features the previously released novella "Spree" which hasn't been available for years. Now "Spree" and this collection of original short fiction has been published together for the first time. *The Silence Between The Screams*, the title story, takes us on a ride with a family that soon discovers that the fabric that makes up our world is not as sound as once thought. That revenge comes in all shapes and sizes in "A Hairy Chest, A Big Dick, and a Harley." Between survival and sacrifice the decisions are decided in "Hymns to Old Gods," and, well, you'll just have to read what this Bram Stoker Award-Winning author, Lucy Taylor, has in store for you.

Also published as a signed limited under the title *A Hairy Chest, A Big Dick, and A Harley* also featuring original cover art by Rick Sardinha. The text is the same, however the limited has many extra features, and interior art.

OVERLOOK CONNECTION PRESS
PO BOX 1934 • HIRAM, GA • 30141
PHONE: 678-567-9777 • FAX: 770-222-6192
EMAIL: overlookcn@aol.com
www.overlookconnection.com

www.ingramcontent.com/pod-product-compliance
Lightning Source LLC
Chambersburg PA
CBHW030234180626
46810CB00008B/3130